SPIDER-MAN®

EMERALD MYSTERY

MARVEL®

EMERALD MYSTERY

Dean Wesley Smith

Illustrations by Bob Hall

MARVEL®

BP BOOKS, INC.

NEW YORK

BERKLEY BOULEVARD BOOKS, NEW YORK

Special thanks to Ginjer Buchanan, John Morgan, Ursula Ward, Mike Thomas, and Steve Behling.

SPIDER-MAN: EMERALD MYSTERY

A Berkley Boulevard Book
A BP Books, Inc. Book

PRINTING HISTORY
Berkley Boulevard paperback edition / October 2000

The BP Books, Inc., World Wide Web site address is:
http://www.bpbooksinc.com

The Penguin Putnam Inc. World Wide Web site address is
http://www.penguinputnam.com

Check out the Ace Science Fiction/Fantasy newsletter,
and much more, at Club PPI!

ISBN: 0-425-17037-3

BERKLEY BOULEVARD
Berkley Boulevard Books are published by The Berkley Publishing Group,
a division of Penguin Putnam Inc., 375 Hudson Street, New York,
New York 10014.
BERKLEY BOULEVARD and its logo
are trademarks belonging to Penguin Putnam Inc.

PRINTED IN THE UNITED STATES OF AMERICA
10 9 8 7 6 5 4 3 2

Chapter One
The Murder

I heard the shots.

One.

Two.

Then once more, as if making a point.

I looked around, hanging upside down, my special webbing holding me tucked under the roof's thick edge, searching for the gun shots' source. I half expected more shots. My stomach twisted for a reason I couldn't figure, but my spider-sense was quiet. At least, I was in no immediate danger.

The sound of a cab plowing through the slush-filled canyon between the buildings of Manhattan. The faint, rhythmic rumble of the subway far beneath the street seemed to echo like low thunder. The streetlights formed ovals of yellow and white on the sidewalks, like round spots on an empty stage.

No human moved on the sidewalks of Forty-second Street.

No more shots cut the air.

I glanced in the direction of the *Daily Bugle* newspaper building, as if I could see it through the swirling snow. Not likely. Thick snowflakes covered my mask.

It was one in the morning.

The delivery of the photos could wait a few more minutes. I still had time to have Peter Parker photos make the morning edition. Enough time for Spider-Man to find the shooter.

Or maybe a body.

With a quick check to make sure my camera and film were still secure in my pouch, I dropped off the ledge, shooting a web at the nearby building so I could swing down the street. Both my hands and feet were cold, but I ignored the feeling. They'd be warm soon enough.

I fought to see any evidence through the swirling snow. I was going on gut instinct more than sight tonight.

The shots came from the street level.

And outside.

That much I could remember.

But where?

I stuck to the side of a brick building and listened again.

No sounds of shouting. No more shots. Nothing.

With thick, falling snow muffling everything, there was no telling exactly where the shots had come from. My spider-sense wasn't warning me of any personal danger, but common sense told me that those shots meant trouble.

As it turned out, big trouble.

I swung back out into the snow to keep searching.

I didn't find the shooter, but two minutes later I did find a body.

The man lay sprawled facedown in fresh snow in a dead-end alley. His arms were outstretched past his head, his legs apart, as if he were trying to make a snow angel, but was a little unsure about the concept. His blood had splattered some, giving the snow around his head a dark look.

I landed about twenty feet up the brick wall above the body, and studied the scene. It was very clear he was dead. I was glad I couldn't see his face right then. I had enough nightmares to live with. I didn't need another.

From the looks of the tracks in the snow, the guy had backed up from near the mouth of the alley, then spun around when hit, ending up sprawled face down in the snow and his own blood.

I moved along the wall to get a closer look at the Dumpster where the dead guy had been.

The snow on the ground by the Dumpster had a circular shape melted into it, as if a hot-plate was under the concrete right there. The dead man's backward footprints started there, and another pair of footprints came from the street, stopped near the melted spot, then went back to the street.

My bet was that the something that had melted that snow had somehow caused the guy to get killed. I had no idea what it might have been.

"Oh, no," a voice said from the street.

I leaned back, trying to blend into the brick wall as best a guy in a red spider suit could blend into a brick wall during a snowstorm.

A figure in a gray trench coat came running into the alley.

A woman.

Since she was focused on the body, she didn't look up to see me.

At first I thought she was going to mess up all the footprints in the snow, but then she veered to the right into a clean, untouched area of the alley. She moved along down the wall to a point past the body, then came in over the dead guy through more untouched snow.

Smart.

More than likely she was a cop.

And good looking, probably. Even with the trench coat and dim light, I could tell her figure could turn its share of heads.

I made a note of the killer's footprints, then looked at hers. Smaller, different markings. Unless she had changed boots, she wasn't the killer.

Big surprise. I had a sneaking hunch that nothing was going to come easy about this murder.

"Oh, no," she said softly. "Bobby."

I now knew the first name of the dead guy.

The woman rocked back and forth on her heels as she knelt beside the body. She didn't touch anything. A normal friend would have tried to touch the body—or vomit out any dinner left in the stomach. She just rocked on her heels, not touching a thing. A real pro. Obviously, she had seen her share of murder scenes along the way.

I silently moved over to a place on the wall above her and the body, then gave her a few more seconds to grieve over someone she clearly knew.

Finally I said, "A friend?"

She was on her feet and had a fairly large gun pointed at me almost faster than I could see. But my spider-sense didn't go off, so I knew she had no intention of pulling the trigger. Not unless I did something really stupid and I had no immediate plans for that.

"Impressive fast draw," I said. "Especially with a trench coat. You practice that?"

"Spider-Man?" The trench-coated woman's voice was low, full, and very rich. In the low light I couldn't tell the color of her eyes, but I would have bet anything they were brown. A deep brown, with gold flakes.

"The one, only, and original friendly, neighborhood one," I said. I eased down the wall until I was eye level with her. I didn't step off the wall. No point in adding more prints to the snow.

I nodded at the body. "You know him?"

The woman looked back at the man with the blood halo. "Bobby Miller. He worked for me."

Her voice was clear, but I could tell she was shaken. Without seeming to even disturb the coat, the large gun disappeared as if she'd been practicing that move for years. More than likely, she had. She was even better than I thought.

"So who killed him?" I asked.

She shrugged and kept staring at the hole in the back of the guy's head as if her gaze might patch it up and he might come back to life. "I don't know," she said after a moment. "The case we were working on shouldn't have been dangerous. He was too young, too eager to help for me to put him on anything that might get him hurt."

The trench-coated woman looked back up at me. Even in the faint light in the alley I could see the intensity in her eyes. Deep, almost insane intensity, driven now by the death at her feet.

"Whoever did this to Bobby," she said, her voice low and cold, "will *pay*."

I let her words hang there in the alley for a moment like a knife ready to cut anything that moved, then backed up the conversation a little. "You said you were working on a case? Police or private?"

"Private," she said. "I used to be a cop. Detective."

She went back to staring at the body.

I let the silence fill the alley again, giving her the time she needed. So she was an ex-detective. She had seen her share of murders. But this one was clearly getting to her. Maybe because the kid was young? Or maybe because the kid had been working for her? It would be interesting to find out the answer.

Finally after a long minute of me hanging on the wall and her staring at the body I said, "About time you call in your old workmates on this one. Before the tracks get covered too much for the police to get anything."

"Yeah," she said, nodding her head as if coming back from a long distance. She did a slow turn, making sure to not mess up any more of the snow than she already had as she studied the crime scene.

I watched her as she focused for a moment on the blood splatters, then stopped her gaze on the area where Bobby had started to back up. I could tell she took in very detail. More than likely she saw stuff I didn't. She was good. Not many cops, ex- and otherwise, when faced with a personal death, would still do their job.

She moved back along her tracks and stopped where Bobby started to back up, studying the area.

I moved along the wall above her. "Something melted the snow there," I said. "My guess is your friend Bobby found something he wasn't supposed to find and it got him killed."

She nodded, then glanced up at me, her brown eyes dark in the dim light. "Thanks."

"Didn't do anything except find the body," I said. "Wish I could have arrived earlier. You got a name?"

"Barb Lightner," she said.

"Office?" I asked.

"Off Lexington on Fifty-second."

"If I find out anything about this I'll let you know." My words surprised me. I guess in the last few minutes I had decided to help her find the killer.

Barb Lightner, private detective, nodded, again staring at the body. "I'd appreciate any help. Now, time for the police."

Following the same path that she took into the alley, she turned and headed back out. I moved quickly along the wall to a place near the front of the alley and watched as she went south toward a nearby twenty-four-hour deli to make the call.

I took a position about six feet up on the wall and snapped a few photos of the crime scene, including two of the melted area in the snow. I figured the *Daily Bugle* might need some photos if this turned out big. And since I had decided to help Barb Lightner find the killer, I might need them for future reference.

The wind swirled the snow as I scrambled back up the side of the building out of the alley. The police had better hurry or there wouldn't be any footprints in that alley left to study.

I shot a web at the vague shape of a nearby building and then swung down through the swirling flakes, heading toward the *Daily Bugle*.

I was long past having any feeling in my feet. My hands were numb globs of flesh on the ends of my arms. I wanted to go home and warm up.

But first I had to develop some pictures.

Chapter Two
Weird Robbers

I hate sweating. Not sure if that hatred has anything to do with my Spider-Man abilities, or just a simple aversion to feeling like a pro wrestler on a bad night. But, I hate sweating.

I also hate standing in lines. Sometimes I think I was born to swing on webs through the man-made canyons of Manhattan, far above the congestion of the streets. The bite from that radioactive spider that gave me my powers was both a curse and a blessing. It gave me the freedom to not always have to spend my life in the crowds.

Standing in lines.

Sweating.

Swinging above the street gave me the realization that there *was* something more than living in the "normal nine-to-five" fashion.

I hated standing in lines. I think I said that. But I couldn't risk making an ATM deposit. With my luck, it wouldn't get posted for two days—or two weeks.

The line in the bank seemed to stretch forever and I had no choice.

None.

Zero.

Zip.

I hated not having a choice. I hated sweating. I hated standing in lines. Seems I hated a lot of things this morning.

The check I'd just picked up from the *Daily Bugle had* to be in my bank account before the day was out, or me in my Spider-Man costume wouldn't be the only thing bouncing around the city tomorrow. I had no choice but to run this errand.

So I stood in the line and sweated and hated just about everything I could think of at the moment.

The bank that was torturing me with a long, slow line was

one of those old-fashioned places built before the turn of the century. It always reminded me of a Grand Central Station for money. Huge marble pillars ran up to an arched ceiling that had been frescoed with a faint star-filled blue sky.

The teller cages were made of polished oak and the offices were glass-enclosed, all neatly kept like showroom windows. As far as I was concerned, a neat office was not an office anyone really worked in. From the looks of the ten offices I could see, no one even entered those rooms.

A grand marble staircase filled the wall opposite from the cages, splitting halfway up to take customers to the upper floors in perfect movie fashion. Only problem with those stairs was each person's every step seemed to echo like a dull tapping of woodpeckers. The tellers must wake up at night screaming from the constant tap-tap-tap-tap.

The massive openness and polished marble floors and columns also made normal talking almost impossible. I always felt I had to whisper when I came in here. Every loud noise echoed and brought a hundred eyes suddenly peering in your direction. In a bank, for some reason, the last thing I wanted to do was bring attention to myself.

All and all, the bank was an impressive place, if you like the feel of an ornate tomb. Mostly I didn't. Of course, standing in line, sweating, I didn't much like anything.

Even in my grumpy mood, I had to admit that in the summer all the marble and rich colors of wood made the bank feel like a nice, cool island surrounded by the humidity and heat outside. However, in the cold winter months the people in charge of the marble structure always cranked up the heat, turning the huge space into something resembling a sauna in a volcano. I half expected to see the columns sweating.

I clutched the check and the deposit slip in my hand like a child holding a note from his parents. At least twenty people were still ahead of me in the main line being serviced by eight tellers. Two or three people ahead of me carried large bags of coins. I was going to be in here for a while longer.

I slipped out of my coat and tucked it under the strap of the backpack that held my camera and film. Then I glanced at my check again just to make sure it was really in my hand. Thank heavens the *Bugle*'s editor-in-chief, Robbie Robertson, had liked the pictures I'd taken yesterday of the big cab riot down on lower Broadway. Half the cabbies in the city were on strike and the other half were working. That created nothing but tension.

Yesterday that tension erupted into a fight. It was really something to see ten cabbies going at each other with fists and clubs in the middle of the street. Robbie hadn't even asked how I'd gotten the overhead shots, just ran three of them on page one.

I had actually done a hand-spring off the ceiling when I saw the pictures in this morning's paper. It meant we had enough money to live for the rest of the month.

But the line at the bank and the heat had killed every ounce of my good feelings. Even taking off the coat hadn't helped much.

Suddenly, my spider-sense started to buzz like an annoying fly in a small room. Danger.

I spun around to face what had to be one of the oddest things I had ever seen. And considering what I've seen over the years, that was going some.

Seven people had entered the bank, single-file and in no hurry. All seven carried handguns pointed straight ahead. But that wasn't what was odd. It was who they were.

Two were elderly women, purses under their arms, winter coats still buttoned. Both clutched small, silver pistols. The two looked more like they should be heading for a church social, or helping their grandkids with getting dressed for school. Not robbing a bank.

Three of the gang were elderly men. One wore a nice overcoat, polished shoes, and a Rolex watch. Clearly rich. The other two seemed more like they were headed for a day of walking in the park, with older coats and snow boots.

The sixth person was a business-type woman, wearing the classic office attire of a bank officer or stockbroker. She even carried a briefcase in her left hand, a gold-plated pistol in her right.

The seventh wore the uniform of an electrical worker, hard-hat and all, right down to the company name on his coat and his name on his chest. "Ray."

They all had blank looks on their faces and different types of pistols in their hands.

I stood there in line, as dumbfounded as the rest of the people in the bank, as all seven simply walked past and right up to seven different tellers' windows, bypassing at least a half hour of standing in line, and shoving the customers at the windows aside.

They simply ignored all of us. Didn't even *look* at anyone, as a matter of fact.

My spider-sense buzzed lightly. Over the years I had learned to read the different levels of my spider-sense warning system. This low buzz was more of a warning.

As the robbers all stopped at the different teller windows, guns pointed at the shocked bank workers, everyone around me in line bolted for the door. A few women screamed, the sound echoing off the marble columns and stairs. I wonder if they even knew they were screaming.

Everyone ran for the doors and no robber tried to stop them.

The armed seven didn't even turn around. Just kept their guns pointed at the shocked tellers.

I quickly moved next to a pillar, stuffed my deposit slip and check deep into my pocket and hauled out my camera. A few pictures of a gang of bank robbers would help pay next month's expenses. Then I'd switch to Spider-Man and stop this craziness.

"Don't move!" a bank guard shouted, his gun pointed at the back of two of the robbers standing at the teller windows. He was a tall guy, with black hair and a long mustache. He wore the uniform of a bank rent-a-cop. I hoped he had a level head on him, or he just might die in this mess.

The buzz of my spider-sense increased slightly.

I snapped a few pictures.

The robbers ignored the guard. The poor guy didn't know what to do. He moved over to a point about where I had been standing in line, took up the classic police-squat-I'm-about-to-shoot-stance and shouted again. "Drop your weapons and turn around!"

That got as much response as his first order.

I clicked a few more pictures.

Not a movement from any of the gang. They just didn't seem to care.

A cop's worst nightmare.

I snapped more pictures.

Outside I could hear police sirens starting to echo through the canyons of the buildings. New York's finest were on their way. It wasn't even going to take Spider-Man to wrap this up. This gang of robbers was pretty bad at the robbery business.

I moved slowly, making sure I snapped a shot of each robber as they stood at the teller windows.

"I said put down your guns!" the guard again shouted, again squatting even lower, as if that would get their attention even more than a shallow squat.

Again he and his squatting was ignored.

He stood back up straight, gun still pointed at the backs of the robbers. I took his picture just for being so brave and stupid as to try to stop seven armed bank robbers.

Behind the cages the tellers' eyes were huge and I could see a bank manager or president shaking his head "No" at the guard. I snapped the manager's picture just for being so smart.

The guard looked as if he was about to burst into tears in shear frustration. He could disobey his boss and shoot all the robbers in the back, but there was no way he was going to do that. At least I hoped he wouldn't do that.

This was the strangest robbery I had ever seen.

Frantically, the tellers filled bags full of money and handed them to the robbers. An old woman with a black handbag and church-Sunday round hat was the first to get her bag of loot.

She turned, gun still pointed ahead, purse slung over one shoulder, bag of money in the other hand like a sack of dirty laundry. Eyes blank and staring straight ahead, she headed for the front door, not even hurrying, or waiting for the other robbers.

I snapped a half-dozen pictures of her. She didn't seem to notice or care.

The guard shouted for her to halt.

She just kept walking.

Outside a police car raced up and slid to a stop in the snow, its lights flashing.

She walked right at it.

I just hoped the police out there had as much restraint and common sense as the guard in here. Otherwise that poor woman was going to end up dead very quickly. But there was no way I could change into Spider-Man in front off all the bank security cameras. I was stuck being Peter Parker for the moment and there was no getting around that.

So I reloaded my camera and kept taking pictures.

Three more robbers finished getting their money and turned for the front door.

"Halt!" The guard shouted again.

The robbers ignored him and me as I snapped away.

The last three finished their robbery and turned to follow the rest of their odd gang. I snapped their pictures, too.

The guard kept his gun leveled at the robbers, but didn't even bother to shout at them. He and I both knew it would do no good. There was no chance he was going to start a blood bath in the bank when they were leaving. Smart guy.

The first older woman reached the glass front entry and headed through into the cold. Outside I could see four cops move into positions, guns aimed at her.

They shouted for her to drop her weapon.

She ignored them also.

She turned and headed up the street.

One smart cop moved over behind her and banged the gun out of her hand. She stopped and didn't fight him at all.

Weird. Really, really weird.

I moved right up to the huge glass front entry, staying a few steps behind the last three robbers, all the time snapping pictures.

As each robber came through the door a policeman knocked the gun out of his or her hand. I got a few great pictures of the procedure.

Behind me the bank tellers and other employees burst into loud cheers as the last robber was caught just outside the door. I moved over to the bank cop and asked his name.

"Steve Kenyon," he said, wiping sweat from his forehead.

"Good job," I said, just as the police burst through the door, guns drawn, ready to take on any more zombie-bank robbers. Luckily for them there weren't any more.

"Thanks," Steve Kenyon said to me as he put his gun away. "Didn't know what to do."

"I'd say not shooting was exactly right," I said.

"Yeah," he said. "I think so, too."

"Going to make sleeping tonight a lot easier," I said, patting his arm.

He only nodded, the shock starting to set in.

Thirty minutes later, after giving my statement to the police, I was in the dark room at the *Daily Bugle* developing photos that would pay most of our expenses for the next month. Great photos of the "Great Zombie Bank Robbery."

In all my years, I hadn't seen Robbie smile as hard as he did when I handed him the photos. Sometimes it didn't pay to be good.

Sometimes it was better just to be lucky.

BROWN EYES

By mid-afternoon, I had gone back to the scene of the crime and deposited my check, then changed to Spider-Man and headed across town. The murder last night in that alley had been bothering me off and on all day. No point in letting it just eat at me like a termite chewing on wood. I'd learned over the last few years that acting instead of waiting seemed to work out more often than not. And on that murder, the best place to start acting was with Barb Lightner, private detective. The snow had stopped and the wind chill was only dropping the temperatures ten degrees or so. Most of the way over to Lexington Avenue, I could actually feel my fingers on my web lines. Unusual for this time of the year.

Barb Lightner's office was in a nice brownstone tucked about a half block off Lexington. I swung down, checked the addresses just outside the door: "Lightner and Associates Investigations . . . 2."

I wondered if one of her "associates" had been Bobby.

I did a quick hop up to the second story window and stared inside. Barb Lightner was sitting with her back to the window, working at a large wooden desk. As far as I could tell, she was alone.

I tapped lightly and she spun around, eyes wide, hand reaching for a drawer in her desk. I had no doubt there was a gun in the drawer she was touching. The woman took no chances and was well trained. Maybe a little jumpy, but after having a friend killed, I'd have been jumpy, too.

"Spider-Man," she said loud enough for me to hear through the glass.

"You're two for two in the identification game," I said, loud enough for her to hear. "But I'm turning into a red popsickle out here."

She jumped to her feet and unlatched the old, wooden-framed window and shoved it open.

I ducked through into the warmth and she slammed the window closed behind me.

Her office was just about what I expected. A big desk, file cabinets, and a leather couch. A couple lamps gave the place a feeling of warmth without taking away from the business part of it. Only her Private Investigator's license was on the wall.

Through an open door I could see an empty secretary's desk in an outer office, a coat rack, plus a few chairs for client waiting. The paintings on her walls out there were of oceans and sun-lit meadows, giving that room even more warmth.

"Afraid of doors?" she asked as she dropped back down into her high-backed leather chair and stared at me.

"Got to keep my reputation up."

She was even more worth staring at in the light than she had been in the dim alley the night before. The night before I'd been wrong about a couple of things. First, her hair wasn't completely brown, but was more a dark blonde, as if the brown in her hair had been slightly colored out. And she was built even better than I had thought. She had full, red lips and wore a tight, white blouse. She was clearly in fine condition. More than likely she spent time at one of the local gyms.

But I was right last night in that dark alley about her eyes. Large and deep brown. And if I looked close, I could see the golden flakes.

"Damn hard making eye contact with you when you're wearing that mask," she said.

I laughed. "Why would you want to look into a spider's eyes?"

"To see if it was going to bite me?" she said.

"I only bite when pushed," I said. Then I shifted the conversation to a much more serious matter. "Any news about Bobby's killer?"

"Nothing at all," she said, sitting back in her chair, disgusted. I could tell the emotion was held in check, but not far under the surface. "We found nothing new at the murder scene. Just the footprints and the melted spot in the snow."

"Exactly what kind of case were you two investigating?"

She frowned at me, as if trying to decide what to tell me. Then she shook her head and leaned forward. "Nothing worth dying for. An owner of an appliance store off Broadway had hired me because he said he suspected employees were ripping him off. He hired me to track it, and I had Bobby standing watch on two possible drop sights the employees might be using."

"The alley?" I asked.

She nodded "That was one of them."

"So one of the employees killed him for a toaster?"

"No," Barb said. "I've already run down all of them. First off, they weren't stealing anything from the owner. The guy was selling his own stuff and pocketing the cash."

"So in case the IRS caught up with the store owner," I said, "he could call it theft and even show he'd hired a private eye to investigate it. Tricky."

"Got it in one," she said, nodding. "An old scam. I've made an anonymous phone call to a friend at the IRS. Figure the guy owes at least that much for getting Bobby killed. I figured it all out this morning. One day sooner and I might have saved Bobby's life."

"What about the accused employees?" I asked, ignoring her opening into punishing herself. "Any chance of leads there?"

"All the ones the owner was accusing were together, with a dozen other eyewitnesses, at a bar when Bobby was killed."

"So that case is a dead-end," I said.

"Totally," she said. "I think you were right when you said Bobby found something and it got him killed."

"But what?" I asked, more to myself than her. "And by whom? You testing the melted area?"

"Yeah," she said, staring at me again. "Both me and the police. I'll have my lab report tomorrow. Why are you so interested in this case?"

"I found the body," I said. "I find the killer, I sleep better at night."

She nodded. "Good to hear spiders sleep."

"I'll check back," I said, turning to go out the open door.

"You're using the door?"

"Number one rule," I said as I reached her office outer door and opened it. "Always keep 'em guessing."

"Wonderful," she said loud enough for me to hear as I went through into the stairwell. "A game show host in a red suit."

I was halfway down the stairs by the time I thought of a good comeback, but yelling it back up the stairs would show no class at all.

A REWARD

The wonderful smell of steak filled the air as I opened the front door of our home in Forest Hills, Queens. Thick steak, with a hint of mushrooms sautéd in butter.

After leaving Barb Lightner's office, I had headed back to the *Bugle*. Robbie had two reporters going after anything they could dig up on the strange bank robbery that morning. All he would say about it was that it was very strange. I could have told him that much. Then Robbie had told me he was going to use at least four or five of my photos for tomorrow's paper, two or three on the front page again. I was on a roll.

And even more importantly, tomorrow I'd have a check big enough to get Mary Jane and me through most of next month's bills. It was like a cloud lifting from my mind, taking along a ton of weight from my shoulders as it went. There was nothing like money worries to cloud a good life. And having those taken away was like having the sun come out after a day of rain.

I had called Mary Jane with the news. From the wonderful smells of the steak and mushrooms, she must have made it out to the store and back since I called. Some days were just better than others.

My beautiful wife was in the kitchen, stirring the mushrooms. I kissed her on the neck and she turned and gave me a hug and kiss.

"So, tiger," she said, pushing me away and going back to stirring the mushrooms as the steak sizzled under the broiler in the oven. "What happened?"

I dropped into a kitchen chair and gave her the rundown of the really strange bank robbery, and how they didn't seem to mind at all that I was snapping their pictures.

"Sounds like they were in some sort of trance," Mary Jane said, shaking her head as she pulled the steaks out.

"That it does," I said. "And even stranger is that none of them looked like they had dressed to go rob a bank."

She laughed. "I had no idea there was a dress code for bank robbers."

"Let me show you," I said. I ducked back into the living room where I'd dropped my pack. I had kept some proof sheets of the photos that hadn't turned out well. They would be good enough to show Mary Jane what I meant by "dressed for a robbery."

I tossed the proof sheets into the middle of the table as Mary Jane handed me an unopened bottle of wine and the opener.

"Wow," I said. "We *are* celebrating tonight."

"Trish?" she said, picking up the proof sheet.

"You know one of the robbers?"

"This is Trish Mathews," Mary Jane said, pointing at the page. "This is no bank robber. She runs the modeling agency I used to work for a few years back. Remember?"

I actually didn't remember. I had enough trouble keeping track of who was doing what crime around the city without keeping up on Mary Jane's old bosses. I glanced at the sheet and where she was pointing. It was the woman dressed as if she were heading to an office, briefcase and all. "That's one of the seven," I said, then went back to working on opening the wine bottle. "Maybe it just looks like your friend Trish?"

My wife frowned, then tossed the proof sheet into the middle of the table before turning back to the stove to finish the steaks. "You're probably right. Trish would have no reason to rob a bank."

I laughed. "From the way those people acted, it didn't seem as if any of them needed a reason beyond wanting to be arrested. It was really weird."

I finished opening the wine and then got that proof sheet off the table and out of sight before my beautiful cook finished filling our plates. There was no way I was going to let a case of mistaken identity ruin a very enjoyable evening.

As it turned out, the next morning in the paper one of my pictures of Trish Mathews was on the front page, with her name under it.

Chapter Three
Method Number Ten

The next day turned out to be just as cold. I could handle the cold. It was the snow that made things hard, especially swinging from one slick building to another. My spider abilities usually didn't fail me on getting a grip, and my webbing worked just as well in cold or hot, but my mind never totally believed I wouldn't slip in the snow. And that slight doubt always kept me slightly on edge when it snowed.

Over breakfast I had promised Mary Jane that I would look into what caused her friend, Trish Mathews, to suddenly become a Bonnie of Bonnie and Clyde fame and stick up a bank. After the wonderful evening we had had celebrating the extra money coming in, I felt it was the least I could do. Amazing how easy a man could be convinced to do something by a woman. Spider-powers or not, I was no exception.

I checked into the *Bugle*, then changed into Spider-Man for the swing across town. No point in fighting the mess in the streets when I could go by air, I always said.

I got to the building housing the modeling agency Trish Mathews owned and changed back to street clothes inside the roof door just slightly before eleven. Six minutes later I was standing in the waiting room of Mathews and Walker Modeling Agency.

I felt instantly out of place, the room was so plush. I mean, deep, thick carpet, don't-be-surprised-to-find-diamonds-in-the-flowers-plush. Soft-looking chairs along two walls looked as if they'd never been sat in and the magazines were arranged so perfectly on the glass end tables, I wouldn't have been surprised if they weren't glued there. It was all the perfect front, just like the models they served up to the public. Just look. Don't touch.

The woman who faced me across the receptionist desk was

beautiful. She had pale, almost pure white skin, wore too much make-up on her eyes, and constantly seemed to be running her fingers through her long brown hair. I put her age somewhere between twenty-two and thirty-two. The sign on her desk said, "Olena."

When I asked to see Susan Walker, Olena sighed and rolled her eyes at me as if I was the stupidest human she had ever met. "No one is seeing Ms. Walker today." Her voice had a high, nasal Brooklyn-from Bensonhurst accent, and I almost laughed at how odd it sounded coming from that model-like face, with that name on the desk.

"I'm sure she will see me," I said, handing her a card Mary Jane had given me with a note on the back. The note basically said that I could help clear Trish Mathews. I wasn't so sure about how successful I would be, but the note at least would get me in the door. "Give this to her."

Without even looking at the card Olena said, "As I was saying, Ms. Walker is not seeing any*body* today." She drew out the word "body" like it was a swear word, dropped the card on her desk, and then ran her right hand through her hair. After all that was finished, she looked directly at me as if she couldn't believe I was still standing there.

Amazing performance. I wanted to applaud.

It looked like it was time for method number ten: *Getting past a really, really stubborn receptionist.* I didn't much like method number ten, but it had never failed me.

I smiled as friendly as I could, then leaned forward so I was slightly too close to her. "If Ms. Walker doesn't see me, you might well be out of a job by noon. Would you like that?"

I doubted I had the power to get her fired, but I knew that if Ms. Walker didn't see me, she wasn't going to be happy when she realized her receptionist had turned me away.

Again I smiled real pretty-like, still leaning over the desk far inside Olena's comfort area. She smelled of bubble gum and lilac hair shampoo.

We held that position for a moment, like a personal-space

standoff, then she blinked and pushed her chair back from the desk slightly.

I had her. She was doomed. I kept leaning forward, keeping the silly smile pasted on my face. I had learned a long time ago that a continuous smile unnerved people, especially when their personal space had just been invaded.

Olena reached in almost under my chin and picked up the card. "I'll give this to her and see what she says. Have a seat."

"I'd rather stand," I said, still smiling as if I was the happiest man alive. I managed to somehow lean in a little farther over her desk.

She gave me a long stare, stood, then a little too fast turned and disappeared through a heavy door behind her desk.

I stood up straight just an instant before I was about to go facedown onto her perfect ink blotter.

Thirty seconds later she came back, looking paler than before, but trying to smile at me. "Ms. Walker will see you now."

She held the door open for me. As I passed her I paused with my nose about an inch from hers. She had her head shoved back hard against the door. I had to admit, up close she had a nice nose. And plucked eyebrows.

Still smiling real, real big, I said, "Thank you."

If she had nodded, she'd have bumped my head. I doubted she'd forget me for some time to come.

Method number ten had worked again.

DEAD END

Susan Walker was a tall woman, taller than I was, and moved like a cat as she came around the end of her desk to greet me. Her hand was firm and warm and she held the handshake the exact right amount of time. I had noticed a lot of women were afraid to shake hands, or didn't realize there was an art to it. Some held it much too short a time and then pulled away.

Other women held on too long, putting too much "meaning" into the handshake. Many men didn't know how to shake hands, either, but Susan Walker did. Perfectly.

"I've heard a lot of very good things about you from Mary Jane," Susan said as she motioned for me to have a seat in a comfortable-looking chair facing her desk. She moved around behind her desk and also sat, leaning forward to show I had her complete attention.

"Thanks," I said, dropping down into the soft cushions. "Mary Jane says a lot of really nice things about you and Trish Mathews, also."

I let that sentence hang in the air for a few quick beats, then asked, "Has Ms. Mathews been released yet?"

"No. No bail yet. Something about the armed robbery charge not allowing it."

The smile and the pink color in her skin drained from Susan Walker's face like water from a sink, replaced by a worried frown and the paleness of shock. Suddenly I could see this was a woman who hadn't gotten much sleep last night.

"Look," I said, "I know you've got to be busy. Mary Jane asked me to look into what happened in that bank. Are you all right with that?"

Susan nodded. "I'm not sure what you can do, but I'm not going to turn down any help at this point. And I'm sure Trish will be grateful also. Only one condition, if you don't mind."

"You name it," I said.

"Nothing I tell you ends up in the paper."

I paused. Even though technically I'm not a reporter, I do have press credentials. And all members of the press have confidential sources. Otherwise they wouldn't get some of the scoops they do—like my Spider-Man "connection." So, right then and there Susan Walker became my "confidential source." I told her, "If anything bad about Trish Mathews ends up in the *Daily Bugle,* it won't be because of me, that's the best I can do."

Susan sighed. "I guess that will have to be enough. What can I tell you that might help?"

"You know, honestly, I don't have the foggiest idea," I thought. And I didn't. I had been right in the middle of that robbery and I couldn't believe it had happened. I had no idea where to even start. And from the article in the paper this morning, neither did the police. It seemed as if none of those robbers should have been there, doing what they were doing.

But they all were. Go figure.

And I had to start somewhere.

"How about some basic questions first," I said. "How was Trish set for money?"

"No problems at all," Susan said. "Not only is this business doing just fine, but her parents left her a great deal of money. She would have no need to rob a bank."

"So we rule that out," I said. "How about what she was planning yesterday? Anything odd?"

Susan shook her head. "Nothing. Trish left here a little after ten in the morning. She was fine when she left. She had a few errands to run and was going to ride the subway to a lunch date with her sister. Instead, before lunch she robs a bank. I just don't understand."

"You're not the only one," I said.

Susan took a deep breath, clearly fighting to keep her strong control about her.

"I assume you've talked to Trish. What does she remember about the entire thing?"

"She remembers getting on the subway and then having the cop handcuff her outside the bank. Nothing at all in between. And I believe her."

"So do I," I said. And I did, even though believing her made no sense. "Maybe she was drugged?"

Susan shook her head no. "They did blood tests. Nothing showed up."

At that we both sat in silence for a few moments, thinking.

Odd didn't even begin to describe this. And I had a sneaking hunch it would get stranger before it got explained.

For a few more minutes we talked about Trish Mathews as a person, getting nowhere. I learned a number of things about her.

She was a good, solid citizen who treated her friends and employees well.

She hated criminals. Gave her time and money to victims organizations.

She was very rich.

She had bought the little gold gun she used in the robbery as protection after a mugging, and usually carried it in a special compartment in her purse. She had a permit for it and had taken lessons with it.

There seemed to be nothing to show she would go so far as to even shoplift, let alone try an armed bank robbery. No wonder Mary Jane had been so upset.

Finally I stood. "If I find out anything useful, I'll let you know."

"Thank you," she said, standing and coming around to my side of her desk.

"Mary Jane's idea," I said. "I'm just trying to help."

She took my extended hand and squeezed it lightly this time before letting it go. Sometimes from a person's touch, you could tell a great deal. I knew Susan really meant her thank you.

In the receptionist area, Olena didn't look up when I said "Bye."

CHARITY CASE

I spent the rest of the morning running down leads on Trish Mathews. I confirmed that what Susan and Mary Jane had told me had been right on the money. Trish just wasn't a person who would rob a bank.

And from what I could figure, there was no missing time in

her morning. From the security people in her office building, I learned that she had left her office exactly thirty-two minutes before she entered the bank.

She dropped off film to be developed at a local photo shop five minutes later, then boarded a subway a block away and got off in front of the bank. Walked straight in and robbed it.

Nothing new or out of place, except the robbery.

Weird. And getting weirder by the moment.

After a quick lunch, I figured it would be better to switch focus for a few hours. The murder the other night in the alley still haunted me and since I was getting nowhere with the favor for my wife, I might as well try to get something done.

I switched to Spider-Man and swung in from the rooftop of Barb Lightner's building, hanging upside down in her window. As the day before, she was sitting with her back to the window, working on some papers.

I knocked, fairly loudly.

Except for a slight jump from being startled, she didn't seem surprised. She didn't even reach for the gun in her top drawer. I must be losing my touch.

She stood and shoved open the window enough for me to come in, ignoring my friendly wave, then slammed it closed.

I moved around and sat facing her on the back of the big chair again.

"Surprised to see you back," she said, dropping into her chair and not looking at me. Instead she looked down at the papers on her desk and pretended to be busy. Her voice was sharp and she seemed angry at me. "I thought you super-hero types had lots of super-villains to chase."

"Oh," I said, "I do. But the super hero union requires me to do a charity case once a year and you're it."

Her head snapped up and she stared at me, her brown eyes slits of anger. I knew she couldn't get an ounce of emotion out of my mask. It gave me the best poker face there was.

After a moment she shook her head and then half-laughed. "I deserved that, didn't I?"

"No problem with being angry," I said. "I've been having one of those days, too. Let's just save it for the person who killed Bobby. What do you say?"

"Deal," she said, her face slightly red. "Sorry."

Time for me to change the subject very quickly. "Are the lab results back?"

"Yeah," she said, flipping me a sheet of paper. It was a report on the area of melted snow. As I read she summarized.

"Radiation melted that snow," she said. "An intense dose of the stuff, but the lab can't figure out what type of radiation. Hell, I didn't even know there were types until today. The fact that the lab can't tell bothers me."

"Bothers me, too," I said. I didn't tell her that I knew a great deal about different types of radiation, thanks to my studies as Peter Parker and a special spider bite.

"I've sent the samples, readings, and a copy of this lab report to a more specialized FBI lab in Washington, DC. But it's going to take them a few days at least to get back to me."

I flipped the report back onto her desk. "So how about, while we're waiting, we check into Bobby's life a little outside his work for you? Maybe something there got him killed."

"We're thinking on the same track," she said.

"Great minds," I said.

"Something like that. I worked on that all last night and this morning. I tracked all of Bobby's movements for the last three days."

"No luck, huh?" I asked, knowing the answer.

"I'd be broke in Vegas," she said. "Bobby didn't seem to have much going outside of school at City College, a few close friends, and working part-time for me. He lived at home with his mother, didn't do drugs, didn't gamble, and only dated once last month."

"There are still people like that? Thought they went out with the fifties."

"Yeah, me too," she said. "Bobby's biggest desire in life

was to be a cop. When he finished city college next spring he planned on applying to the academy."

I didn't know what to say to that. Actually, there was nothing I could say. The kid had lead a boring, sane life, with dreams the size of a small apartment. But they were still his dreams and it had been his life. And that was worth something. He should not have died the way he did.

No one should die that way.

Right then I knew I would be spending a lot more time than I had planned on finding out who killed Bobby.

ANOTHER DEAD END

Barb gave me the name of one of Bobby's friends. A red-headed kid named Josh. I found him about an hour later and for the next three hours, right on through the rush hour, I tailed the kid like a shadow.

He did nothing unusual, nothing illegal, nothing outside of going to a class, then catching a subway to a small cafe where he met three other students to study for a very long, very boring hour, then to a job waiting tables at a little Italian place off Fifty-second.

After those hours of watching him, I knew without a doubt that Josh had no more idea why Bobby was killed than I did. And hadn't been a part of it in any way. In fact, he was very much as I imagined Bobby had been: a good kid. Luckily for all of us, there were a lot of them around. They just didn't make the news like the bad ones.

Around seven I had forgotten what my fingers felt like, they were so cold. And it had started to snow again. Thick flakes that stuck to my mask a well as the street and building roof-tops.

I watched it start to snow as I hung upside down under the roof ledge of the building across from the restaurant Josh worked at. I had just spent an entire day on two different projects and got absolutely nothing done. I'd been frustrated a lot in the past, but I know I couldn't remember a day that felt much more frustrating than this one.

"Time to go home," I said aloud into the flurry of snow flakes. The thought of our warm house and the smells of Mary Jane's wonderful cooking sent me dropping from the ledge as if my grip had suddenly failed.

I fired a web across the street and swung up onto the top of a nearby building. A few minutes later I was inside the *Bugle*, heading down the stairs as Peter Parker, ready to make my commute home to a warm meal and a good night's sleep.

I had no idea, right at that moment, that it would be the last good night's sleep I would get in a long, long time. If I had, I would have appreciated it much more than I did.

Chapter Four
Life Gets Weird

Robbie Robertson's office at the *Daily Bugle* always made me feel comfortable for some reason. It was a place where I knew I was welcome and my talents appreciated. Again this morning Robbie had run another of my photos from the bank robbery on page one, only this time with the caption: "Nothing Makes Sense In Robbery."

I couldn't have agreed more. Nothing did make sense. And even though it was early, and Robbie's office was my first stop of the day, I could already feel the frustration of the situation starting to build.

The newsroom of the *Bugle* was in what I call its "low-energy" mode. A lot of people were scattered around the computers and desks, working and talking. But the room didn't have that frenetic motion of a newspaper on deadline. That would happen later, just as it did every day.

I knocked on Robbie's door and went in when he motioned through the glass for me to enter. His office was off the newsroom, with a large window overlooking the city on one side and another large window looking across the newsroom on the other. I always thought the room symbolic for the person who ran the *Bugle*. One face looking at the city, one face running the paper.

Right now, outside Robbie's window, it was snowing lightly. Cold, small flakes that didn't seem to want to land anywhere. The kind of snow that made a person feel good being inside a nice, warm office.

Robbie was talking on the phone. I dropped into the big leather chair facing his desk and turned so I could put my feet up over the arm. That was the most comfortable place in the entire building.

"Peter," Robbie said, hanging up the phone and leaning

forward over his desk to look at me directly, "you were there. Can you make any sense of that bank robbery?"

"Good morning to you, too," I said.

He smiled and waited for me to answer his question, his dark eyes staring at me. All business.

"No, I can't," I said. "I spent part of yesterday trying to find anything that made sense about those events and came up with even less than I understand about national politics."

Robbie sighed and leaned back in his chair, his large hands tucked behind his head. "Weird," he said, and then again let out a long sigh.

I was hearing that word a lot when this robbery was talked about.

"Yesterday," I said, "at my wife's request, I investigated one of the robbers. Trish Mathews. Mary Jane used to work for her and swore Mathews couldn't be a bank robber."

"Rich, good-looking one who owns the modeling agency?" Robbie asked, clearly interested.

"The one and the same," I said. "Didn't actually talk to her, but did spend some good time with her friend and partner."

"And . . . " Robbie said, shoving me to go on.

"Mathews is the type that would never think of robbing a bank. Period. Not one doubt at all. She had no need of the money. She also has no memory of the event."

"None of them do," Robbie said. "And none of them are anything more than normal people in one way or another."

"So we need to find what turned them all into bank robbers," I said. "What did they all do before the robbery that was the same? I tracked Mathews from the moment she left her apartment to the moment she went into the bank. Anyone done that for the others?"

"More than likely the police have," Robbie said, sitting forward in his chair and making some notes as he talked. "But not a bad idea for us to get the information too, and compare them across."

Behind me there was a knock on Robbie's door and a young intern with a fresh face and too many earrings entered without waiting for an invitation. She wore baggy pants and a shirt that hung on her like a loose towel.

"Weird guy with dead eyes gave me this to give to you." The intern dropped a paper on Robbie's desk and turned to go.

"Wait," Robbie said.

The kid stopped, but clearly didn't like being there.

Robbie read the note, then glanced up at the intern. "What did the guy look like who gave you this?"

"Suit," the intern said. "Black briefcase, bad gold tie. And dead-eyes, like a bad movie. He handed the note to me in the lobby, like I look like a messenger or something."

I didn't bother to tell the earring-covered kid that was exactly what she looked like, and that being a messenger was part of her job description on top of that. No point.

"Thanks," Robbie said and the intern left.

"You know," I said, "the kid just described the same look the robbers had in the bank yesterday. The 'walking dead look,' I would call it."

Robbie flipped me the note and said nothing until I read it. It was on yellow legal paper and had been folded a few times. In the very center of the page were typed the words:

I am the Jewel. I am in charge of the crime in this city. No one should stop my people. Be warned.

It wasn't signed. I read it twice, then tossed it back to Robbie. "Another letter for the nut case file."

"More than likely," Robbie said, "but that description of the guy who delivered it bothers me."

"Yeah, me too," I said. "But that description fits a tenth of the city's population and half of the cab drivers."

Robbie smiled. "Perfect reason to waste a reporter's time on it, don't you think?"

As I laughed, he flipped a switch on his intercom. "Send in Betty Brant."

With that I stood and headed for the door. "Pictures to take, boss."

"Keep me informed if you find anything," Robbie said.

"You'll be the first," I promised as I headed out his door and across the busy news room. I would keep that promise if I could. I liked working for Robbie. And I liked the money he paid me for my pictures. But I doubt he'd much care for a picture of what I had in mind doing the rest of the day.

A death of a young man in an alley was eating at me. Before I went another step farther, I had to do what I should have done yesterday. It was time to discover who Barb Lightner really was, not just who she said she was.

Maybe it was something she had done that had gotten Bobby killed.

I hoped not, but I had to be sure.

INVESTIGATING THE INVESTIGATOR

The snow had stopped again and the day was one of those cold, gray things that seemed to fill a lot of my memories of winter. The light filling the canyons between the buildings made everything just dull and sort of muted.

As Spider-Man, I swung over to the Midtown South Precinct and waited under a roof ledge across the street. I knew Sergeants Drew and Hawkins had no normal return time to the station. But since I'd called and they were out, I figured they had to return at some point. I'd give them an hour or so and then go see if I could find them before going home for dinner. As it turned out, I only had to wait about forty-five minutes before they showed up.

They both looked like normal city detectives, rough in the face, bad dressers, slightly overweight in the stomachs. Today both wore gray overcoats and fedora-like black hats. But I knew these two were members of the white-hat good guys club. They had proven themselves to me a number of times over the last few years. By and large I trusted them, as much as anyone could trust a city detective.

I swung down and landed on the brick wall of the Midtown

South Precinct headquarters as they started up the short flight of stone stairs for the door.

"Can I borrow your shoe," Drew said to Hawkins without missing a step. "There's a spider I want so smash."

"You're not getting that red gunk on my new loafers," Hawkins said. "These things cost me forty bucks."

Neither of them stopped or even broke pace up the stairs toward the front door.

I shook my head. I was having one of those days when no one felt like saying a simple hello.

"Barb Lightner?" I said.

That stopped both about five steps in front of me like I'd sprayed them with quick-drying cement.

Hawkins tipped back his hat and looked up at me. "What's she to you?"

"Body in the alley two nights ago? First name of Bobby?"

Both nodded and said nothing.

These two could see through a lie even with my face covered, so I figured the best thing to do was tell them the truth. "I was there when she found the body. Thought I'd look into it a little, maybe help you and her find the killer."

"And why would you do that, wall-crawler?" Hawkins asked.

I shrugged. "Just call it my good deed of the year. From what I've heard, you two could use all the help you can get."

"Pest control help," Hawkins said.

"Yeah," Drew said. "You're a real boy scout."

"Just forgot to wear my uniform today," I said.

"So you a witness?" Hawkins asked.

"If I were," I said, dropping down and facing the two policemen, moving up fairly close to them, "the murderer would be in jail right now and we wouldn't be having this conversation." I put a lot of coldness in the last part of that sentence.

Drew nodded. "Yeah, I suppose he would."

"So," Hawkins said, "let me guess. You want information about Barb Lightner, just to make sure it wasn't something she did that got Bobby killed. Right?"

"On the money," I said, impressed at the question. My respect for Hawkins went up another notch.

"We already looked into it," Drew said, "just to cover the routine. Barb is as clean as they come."

"You know her story?" Hawkins asked me.

"Met her in the alley for the first time, then twice in her office to check out details. I know she used to be a cop is all."

"Detective First Class," Hawkins said. "She used to be our boss, actually. Best there was working here."

"Second that," Drew said. "That was back in the days when you and the police weren't so friendly."

"Remember well," I said.

"Husband got killed in a stupid mugging," Hawkins said. "About two years ago. We couldn't find a thing, so she quit and set up her private detective office to spend all her time tracking the guy."

"So that's what she and Bobby were working on that night?" I asked.

"No way," Hawkins said. "She caught the creep who killed her husband over a year ago. Didn't come back to being a cop, though. She felt she could do more good where she was at. She helps us a lot on some cases."

"Yeah," Drew said. "I'd like to pay her back on this one. Find the scum who killed the kid."

"The case she was working on was nothing more than a furniture scam case," Hawkins said.

"Yeah," Drew said. "We got the guy behind that in lock-up now. It has nothing to do with the kid's death in that alley. I'm sure of that."

"So am I," Hawkins said.

"And I suppose you won't tell me if you have any leads?" I asked.

"Probably not," Drew said.

"If we had any," Hawkins said. "All we got is footprints, the type of gun that killed him, and that stupid melted spot. None of it goes anywhere yet. How about you?"

"Exactly nothing," I said. "But you two will be the first to know when I do."

"Yeah, right," Drew said, smiling for the first time. "And it's going to be ninety degrees in the shade tomorrow afternoon." With that they both started for the door.

"I'll tell Barb you two send your love," I said, firing a web at the building across the street.

"She wouldn't believe you," Hawkins said, pulling open the front door of the precinct building. "She knows us."

They were inside before I could think of a snappy comeback.

I headed back toward the *Bugle*. I just needed a little more before I could completely trust Barb Lightner. Not that I didn't trust her already, but I had learned a long time ago it was always better to be safe than sorry.

MORE ZOMBIES

For the next three hours I looked up everything I could find in the *Daily Bugle* records and morgue on Barb Lightner and the death of her husband. By the time I was done I knew that the two sergeants had told me the truth about what had happened with Barb. And also about how good she was as a cop. There was nothing she had done, outside of hiring Bobby on a seemingly safe case, that had gotten him killed. That much I was sure of.

I went up to the roof to change into Spider-Man to swing home, but something made me look outside first. It was snowing so hard, I could hardly see across the roof top. No way was I going to try swinging through that if I didn't have to. It was the subway for me tonight.

For some reason, down on the sidewalks, the snow seemed to be doing more swirling around the people than falling. It made it a little easier to walk. Not much, but a little. At least this way it wasn't clogging up my mask. And my hands were staying nice and warm inside my coat pockets.

I was about to turn down into the subway stairs when my spider-sense gave a buzz. Not the "move-or-die" warning, but more of the "danger-nearby" type.

Then a woman shouted, "Robbery!"

About thirty paces away through the snow I could see a man holding a gun facing a ticket window of a theater.

The woman who had shouted was backing away, along with her boyfriend. A number of others had stopped on the sidewalk. Quickly a wide ring of people was starting to form around the man holding the gun.

Inside the cage, the woman ticket seller was scrambling to put money into a bag that had held her hamburger a few moments before.

The guy with the gun wasn't moving. Instead, he was just standing there, pistol pointed at the window, ignoring everyone around him as if they weren't there.

My spider-sense was telling me this wasn't very dangerous, just as it had done at the bank. And everything about it looked odd. As odd as the bank robbery.

"Another zombie robbery," I said to myself.

I grabbed my camera from my backpack and moved quickly up through the crowd, snapping pictures one right after another as I went. I would be lucky if any of them came out, considering the swirling snow and people, but it was worth the attempt.

As I got inside the group of gawkers, it became even clearer this robber was exactly like the ones in the bank. He was wearing a nice overcoat and had expensive-looking boots. His hand holding the gun was covered with a leather driving glove and his hat was fur-lined. Not your typical robber clothes.

I snapped two quick pictures, tucked the camera away in the pack, then moved up beside him. I didn't normally get involved in stopping a crime as Peter Parker, but at the moment I didn't have the time or the place to change into Spider-Man. So Peter was going to be the hero.

"I really don't think you want to do this," I said to the man.

He didn't look at me or even move. The gun remained level, pointing at the ticket seller.

She was about twenty, with huge, brown eyes and the look on her face of a deer caught in a truck's headlights. She kept swallowing over and over, as if taking a bad-tasting medicine and not getting it down.

"Duck," I told her.

"What?" Through the glass her voice sounded a great deal like a squeak.

"Duck under your counter now," I said as forcefully as I could. "And stay there until I say come up."

The man with the gun didn't move or say a word.

Her eyes got even wider for an instant and then she ducked behind her counter.

With a quick smack on the man's wrist, I knocked the gun into the snow.

"What?—what—let me go!"

The guy was coming back to his old self. This was going to be interesting.

"Would one of you please call a cop," I said to the stunned crowd who had watched me disarm the man. Then I glanced at the ticket window. "And miss, you can stand up now. All clear."

Slowly her brown eyes peered over the edge of the counter, then she stood up, smiling real big.

"Better buzz for your manager," I said

She nodded, still smiling and looking very relieved.

Thirty minutes later I had given my story to the police and was headed back to the *Bugle* to develop the pictures. With luck I'd have another few shots in the morning edition as a reward for my good deed. At this rate Mary Jane and I were going to have enough for the next few months' bills.

I didn't make it any farther than the door to the news room. The police scanner was squawking like the world had exploded. And it seemed it had.

All over town people and places were getting robbed.

I spent all of ten second making sure I had two locations in my mind, then headed for the roof. Spider-Man was going to be working tonight.

And work I did.

My first stop, about three blocks from the *Bugle,* I webbed a gun from the hands of a sixty-year-old woman holding up a deli in front of sixty people.

Two blocks to the east I snatched another gun out of the hands of a woman in a nurse's uniform and white shoes holding up a newsstand.

It kept going like that, one after another. By far, it was the strangest night I had spent in a long time. Even though the robbers held guns, my spider-sense kept telling me there was no danger. By my count, I stopped over thirty perfectly ordinary citizens as they attempted to rob one place or another.

It was also one of the coldest nights I could remember spending outside. The snow never let up, and after midnight, the wind kicked up too, making it even more impossible to see. Usually I loved swinging freely through the air, moving around between the city's buildings. But tonight I spent most of my time on walls, under overhangs near police cars, listening to police scanners. That way I only had to swing to the next crime when it was called in. Doing that also managed to maintain some feeling in my fingers. But I lost the feeling in my toes sometime around midnight.

It wasn't until just after seven in the morning that everything changed. And not for the better.

I was tucked in under the awning of a department store, listening to the police scanner as a nearby cop finished up the paperwork on an accident. There hadn't been another zombie robbery in almost a full hour, and I was hoping it had stopped for the moment. I couldn't be that lucky.

The police radio crackled to life and the dispatcher reported a robbery happening three blocks from my position, over near the lower end of Central Park. I fired a web across the street and swung up and out. It only took me a few more long swings, even in the swirling snow, to get to the side of a building above the park, a place where I could see what was happening.

About fifty paces from me a man in a rumpled hat and jacket was holding a gun on a delivery man, who had his arms in the air and had backed against the side of his truck. A dozen people stood nearby, watching, hanging back out of harm's way.

There didn't seem to be anything to rob from the delivery truck, so I had no idea what the robber wanted. So far all the zombie robberies had been to get money, although no money in any of them had been lost.

"Don't shoot," the delivery man begged, his hands flailing over his head.

The robber just stood there and said nothing.

Suddenly my spider-sense went wild.

I fired my webbing at the man with the gun. I would be lucky to hit him from this distance, but I had to try.

He just fired. For no reason.

My aim was right on the money. My webbing hit the pistol, clogging it. Unfortunately, as good as my aim was, my timing was poor. The delivery man was down. I could only hope he wasn't dead.

As I jumped to his side, shouting for someone to call an ambulance, he sank down into the snow, his red blood splattering over the whiteness.

"Spider-Man," he gasped.

"Right here," I said. "Try not to talk. Help's on the way."

I looked up at the people surrounding us. One woman said, "Someone went to call an ambulance."

I nodded my thanks to her.

"Why did he shoot me?" the driver asked.

"I don't know," I said, pressing over the wound to try to slow the bleeding. "I honestly don't know."

The guy tried to laugh, but it came out as a choking sound. Not a good sound. Then he managed to say, "Neither do I."

Chapter Five
Common Factor?

I finally dragged my corpse-cold and dog-tired body into the house a little after eight in the morning. Mary Jane was sitting at the kitchen table, reading the morning paper, breakfast dishes scattered in front of her. I hadn't pulled an "all-nighter" in months. Every time I did, I swore I wouldn't do it again. I wasn't as young as I used to be.

She glanced up, gave me a warm smile that I felt all the way to my fingers. But it would take more than a smile to get to my frozen toes. She led me by the hand in under a hot shower. By the time I got out, the wonderful smell of frying bacon filled the air. It reminded me that I hadn't had dinner the night before. Such a crazy night, I had simply forgotten. I used to do that a lot, but the last year or so I had managed to keep better track.

The shower had thawed my toes, made me feel almost human again. Breakfast helped. Between bites I managed to tell Mary Jane about the night, right up to the shooting of the delivery man this morning.

It turned out the shooter was a janitor at a nearby building on his way to work. He had no criminal record and no memory of even getting off the subway, let alone shooting a guy. The delivery man was working a flower route, with no money in his truck. None of it made any sense.

Luckily, the janitor was such a bad shot, he had only winged the delivery man.

"Wow," Mary Jane said. "Can you imagine heading to work like a normal morning and the next thing you remember, you've shot a man and have been kicked into a snow drift. How weird that must seem."

"It would drive me nuts, that's for sure."

"Yeah, me too," she said. "So Trish isn't the only one caught in this insanity."

"No. At least a hundred are now, after last night."

"A hundred?" Mary Jane said, shocked.

"Yeah, at least that. And my guess is there will be more before it's over. It seems anyone can become one. I've got to find out what is causing this and get it stopped quick. Too many decent people are getting hurt."

"Any ideas at all?"

I shook my head. I honestly didn't have a clue. I'd been stopping the crimes all night. The only pattern I could see was that they were just normal people suddenly turning to crime and not even knowing they were doing it.

Or remembering why.

"You know," Mary Jane said, taking a corner off a piece of the toast she'd fixed for me and munching on it. "It almost seems as if they are being drugged. Is that possible?"

"Anything is possible at this point. But none of the bank robbers, including Trish, showed any signs of a drug—odd or otherwise—in their systems. I would imagine the police are testing everyone from last night and this morning."

She nodded. "How about hypnosis?"

"Like the Ringmaster from the Circus of Crime?" I said, remembering one of my first foes. I thought for a moment, remembering how he would use hypnosis to rob people, then shook my head. "Not unless it's a very weird form of it," I said. "People under hypnosis don't do things they wouldn't do in real life. I doubt if Trish would have ever pointed a gun at a bank teller. Then there's the amount of people. The Ringmaster *could* hypnotize whole crowds, but this sounds more random."

"Maybe it's a disease of some sort," Mary Jane said, then laughed at her own joke.

"Yeah, the twenty-minute robbery flu."

She smacked my arm for the bad joke. I deserved it. There really wasn't anything funny about what was happening. And now that one of the zombie robbers had actually pulled a trigger, I had a hunch things were going to get worse until I got to the bottom of this mess.

"I'd say look for the common factor among all the rob-bers," Mary Jane said. "Something before they did the crimes. There has to be something there. You've got enough of them now to find some sort of pattern that way, don't you?"

"Yeah," I said, pushing the empty plate away. "I do. But that's going to take more time than I have, especially if I'm spending it stopping them."

"Can't Robbie put some reporters on it?"

"Good looking," I said, "you are full of some great ideas this morning. Robbie and I already got that ball started yesterday."

"No sleep, huh?" She gave me a smile.

Twenty minutes later, after a very long "good luck" kiss from my beautiful wife, I was headed back to the *Daily Bugle* with fresh fluid in my web shooters and a dry Spider-Man cos-tume on. At least the snow had stopped for the moment. Maybe that was a sign today would be a better day?

I could only wish.

GOING FOR HELP

My first stop was Barb Lightner's office. Not because I wanted to find out if she had discovered anything more about Bobby's killer, but to ask her for help.

She had on her coat and was standing near her office door when I knocked on her window. She looked up and actually frowned at me.

"Well, I'm glad to see you, too," I said, but I doubt my words got through the glass.

She opened the window for me and I bounced in. I was about to walk to the chair when I realized my feet were snow-covered. So I just stood instead. She looked as if she was in a bad enough mood without me making it worse by tracking on the floor.

"Make it quick," she said. "I've got an appointment."

"No luck, huh?"

"You come to give me a hard time or do you have something I need to know?" Her dark eyes were like sharp points cutting at me. This was one woman I didn't want really mad at me. Just annoyed was bad enough.

"I've got nothing new about Bobby's case," I said.

She started to turn to the door.

"Wait," I said. "I came to ask for your help on something else."

Now that stopped her.

She turned back and stepped toward me. "And just how can I help *you,* the great Spider-Man?"

"How about giving me a break and listening to what I've got to say?"

She took a slight step back as if I'd actually slapped her, then nodded. "Sorry, I was on my way to a memorial service for Bobby."

That felt as if she had slapped me. I had been so wrapped up in the problems of the zombie robberies, it hadn't dawned on me today would be the funeral. How stupid could I get?

"Bad timing on my part," I said, holding up a hand as if I was asking for peace. "Really sorry. I can come back."

She waved my comment off. "I'm early." She took off her coat and tossed it over the corner of her desk, then faced me, arms folded. "I'm listening."

"Thanks," I said.

It took me about two minutes to quickly go over the bank robbery and the long night of crime last night, ending with the delivery man getting shot.

Then I got to the point. "Something is getting to these inno-cent people and I need your help backtracking some of them. A trained investigator like you might be able to see a detail or two that I might miss."

She nodded, thinking. I could also tell her understandably bad mood had melted some.

"Anything would help at this point," I said. "It was really ugly out there last night."

She looked at me. I doubted that I made a very needy sight

in my Spider-Man costume, but I tried to look like the needy type.

"Tell you what," she said after a moment of staring at me with those dark, piercing eyes. "After the service I'll check in with Drew and Hawkins, see what they've put together, get a few names and see what I can come up with."

"Thank you," I said.

She picked up her coat. "Check back with me here about seven tonight."

"Thanks," I said and moved to the window, sliding it open. I jumped up on the sill and looked back. "You want to lock up behind me?"

"Why?" she said. "You're the only one who uses the second-story window. I doubt locking it is going to keep you out."

With that she turned and headed toward the elevator.

I closed the window behind me, not really sure if it was colder inside or outside.

ANOTHER NOTE

"Peter!"

Robbie's voice echoed over the natural hum and talking of the news room. I had been standing next to the police scanner to see if any more zombie robberies were happening. Luckily, they had stopped for the moment.

I glanced at where he stood in his office door and he waved for me to join him.

A few moments later I dropped down into my favorite chair facing him across his desk. Behind him through his big window I could tell it hadn't started snowing again. He tossed me another folded piece of yellow legal paper.

"Same nut?" I asked, unfolding the paper.

At a glance I answered my own question. This note was as simple as the last one, typed in the same fashion.

I am responsible for the rash of robberies by what your paper calls "Zombies." No one can stop me or my zombies. I control the city. If you do not believe me, go to Central Park, near the skating rink at noon. I will prove it to you.

It was signed *The Jewel.*

"This guy is starting to creep me out," I said, flipping the note back on Robbie's desk.

"So, do I believe the note or not?"

"Anyone can take credit," I said. "We're making no secret of the fact no one knows what's happening."

"True," Robbie said, picking up the yellow paper and studying it again. "But after last night, people are starting to get scared."

"It's scaring me," I said. And it was. If someone could control regular people without their seeming to know about it, then maybe this person could control me. And someone crawling up inside my head and yanking my chains bothered me a lot.

"Yeah, scares me too," Robbie said.

I could tell he wasn't just saying that.

"You want to be near the skating rink around noon just to be sure?" Robbie asked, tossing the yellow paper into the basket on his desk. "Something happens and I'll give that and the first note to the police."

"No problem," I said. "Good little deli right near there I can have lunch."

"Thanks. After last night I have all the reporters working on other things at the moment."

"So, any patterns emerging from what our zombies did before they pulled guns?"

"Nothing," Robbie said. "And from what I can gather, the police don't have anything either."

"There's something," I said, trying to sound more sure than I felt. "We're just not finding it."

"Hope you're right," Robbie said.
I hoped I was too.

GUNFIGHT IN CENTRAL PARK

The day was turning into another of those gray, cold winter days, where you could just feel the snow in the air over you, like a giant pillow about to be dropped. But at the moment at least, it still wasn't snowing. Me and my toes could be thankful for that.

Central Park's Wollman Rink is in a depresion in the southern part of the park. It's also surrounded by evergreens. Setting up my camera would be tricky. But I managed to find a good spot on one of the larger evergreens.

On one hand, I was convinced that nothing was going to happen. At the same time I was glad Robbie showed me the note. Most nuts who wrote threatening letters to the paper turned out to be harmless quacks, usually living in their own fantasy worlds. Every time there was an unsolved crime, at least two or three people would write the paper or the police claiming credit. I never did understand what made such people do that, but there were psychology books full of reasons. I just figured this was another of those idiots.

However, since I had absolutely no other leads, being here made as much sense as anything else at the moment. Except maybe being home in bed, getting some much needed rest.

I stood on the tree limb next to my camera, watching the traffic in the park and through the branches on the nearby street. Since it was a regular business and school day, the skating rink wasn't too crowded. It would be later, that's for sure. But the street was busy with noon traffic, and so was the sidewalk running beside the park.

All seemed normal. Very normal, actually.

I glanced at the clock on the skating rink lodge. Thirty seconds until noon. There was the normal lunch traffic fighting its way between mounds of snow on the street. People were filling the sidewalks, walking carefully on the slick surfaces. Skaters below me on the rink.

Winter in the city. Nothing unusual.

Until about twenty people around the rink and on the park sidewalk suddenly stopped in their tracks. My spider-sense went wild.

Pulling guns out of pockets and purses, they moved like movie zombies as they took cover behind different things.

A large, overweight woman wearing a loud red coat tried to hide behind a small light pole as she aimed a small pistol at a man squatting behind a garbage can.

Two men sort of shoved at each other to take cover behind a bench. Both had guns. Finally, one turned and moved to a nearby snowdrift.

Five took cover behind trees far too thin to give much cover.

Another six or seven moved over behind bushes.

One woman with a gun even stood behind a park rules sign that was no more than an inch wide.

It was so surreal that it took me a moment to realize what I was seeing. Like a slow-motion dance, twenty or so normal people had drawn guns and went for cover. They were going to have a gunfight right here beside the skating rink in Central Park.

I tapped the start button on my camera and dove for the ground below, hoping I could get those guns before disaster hit.

Almost as if there had been a countdown, at exactly the same instant every person with a gun opened fire at another person with a gun.

It sounded as if I was jumping into the middle of a hundred firecrackers as the entire string went off. My spider-sense was going wild.

I rolled and dodged as two bullets almost cut me off at the knees. I used my webs to yank one gun out of a man's hand, then another web shot to clear a gun form a woman's hand.

I couldn't remember when I had moved so fast before, but I

couldn't remember the last time I was in the middle of an all-out gunfight, either.

I yanked the gun from the woman in red and flipped it into the snow, then an instant later I got two guns at the same time from two men behind snowdrifts.

My spider-sense warned me to duck and I did, rolling hard behind an overflowing trash can while covering another man's gun with a shot of webbing, then yanking it away.

One after another, I disarmed the zombies as the echoes of their shots slowly died off the nearby trees.

Finally I got the last gun from the hands of a taxi driver hiding behind a sidewalk bench. He was out of ammunition, but was still clicking away.

I glanced around.

As far as I could see, no one had been hit, which was a pure miracle since at least a hundred rounds had been fired before I got it stopped. Luckily it seemed these zombies were the worst shots on the planet.

On the nearby footpaths regular pedestrians were slowly climbing to their feet and helping others up out of the snow where they had taken cover. It was just flat lucky that no wild or stray shots had hit anyone. But it seemed no one was bleeding or staying down on the ground.

Lucky.

Very, very lucky.

This could have been a blood bath. It was intended to be.

The letter writer who called himself "The Jewel" was the real thing after all, it seemed. At least now there was a lead and a name. That was more than anyone had just a few minutes before.

Then I realized how really, really odd everything around me still was.

Instead of having twenty dazed and confused people who seemed to have just woken up, all the people I had disarmed still thought they had guns in their hands. Yanking the real guns out of their hands hadn't been enough to snap their walking trance.

They were still pointing imaginary guns at each other and pulling imaginary triggers, like children playing soldier with their friends. None of them were even moving to pick up a nearby real gun.

I stood in the middle of the imaginary gunfight and just stared as twenty normal adults hid behind something and pretended to shoot at another person.

The crowd grew around it all, talking quietly at first, then slowly starting to laugh—a nervous, hysterical noise.

The gunfighters kept firing their imaginary guns.

The crowd laughed louder. The sight broke the tension of the terror they had felt just a few moments earlier. There was no joy in their laughter, but they were happy to be alive.

If this wasn't what Rod Serling had imagined the *Twilight Zone* to be, I didn't know what was.

Chapter Six
He Likes to Watch

The snow held off all day, hanging over the head of the city like a huge, gray hammer waiting to pound down. The streets felt quiet, as if the white drifts shoved aside by the plows muffled the sound. Or maybe it was just the city waiting, holding its collective breath, wondering who would become a zombie next.

Since the shoot-out in the park, no one had. At least not that I knew of.

I spent the first two hours after the shoot-out at the *Bugle*, developing and enlarging pictures for Robbie. So it just so happened I was in his office again, with him looking over my pictures, when the third note from "The Jewel" arrived.

Robbie went through the same routine, asking the messenger, a young girl named Hailey, where she had gotten the note.

Hailey, who wore clothes that looked like they might fall off at any moment because they were so loose and baggy, was a journalism major down at City College and interned at the *Bugle* two days a week. Over the past few months she'd done a couple errands for me without complaint and as quick as she could. I liked her.

It seemed this third note was handed to her by a woman dressed in a heavy winter coat and wearing jeans. The woman had a dead look in her eyes that had "spooked" Hailey. Or, as Hailey said, "She was like creepy, man."

"Zombie delivery service," I said.

Hailey wiped her hands on her baggy pants, a wide-eyed look on her face. "You don't think it's catchin', do you?"

I shrugged. "Better wash real good just to make sure."

Like a flash Hailey was out the door.

Robbie frowned at me.

He read the note, holding it by the upper right corner only, then handed the standard yellow paper to me to read. I held it by the same corner. I doubted the police would be able to pull any prints off of it, but no point in making the process even more confusing.

Now you know I am real. The crimes will continue for as long as I want them to. Only I can stop them.

It was again signed, *The Jewel* in block letters.

"That's a lot of help," I said, dropping the note back on Robbie's desk.

"Yeah," Robbie said and picked up his phone. Thirty seconds later he had informed the police to come get the note.

I waited until he was finished, then tried a summary of the situation out on him. "Let me get this straight. We've got a nutcase who can turn normal people into zombies to try to rob and kill other people, yet the nutcase gets nothing out of it. Right?"

Robbie nodded. "That's what's happening. But there has to be a reason."

"Exactly what I've been struggling with. Why do this?"

"Control?" Robbie asked, pointing at the letter. "He just likes controlling other people."

"More than likely," I said. "Which doesn't help us at all."

"Not until we find the point he's taking his zombies under control," Robbie said.

Robbie and I sat there in silence for a moment, both thinking. Then it dawned on me what Robbie had said. Controlling another person would have no value either unless . . . "Maybe he gets his kicks watching."

Robbie nodded. "Try blowing up some of those pictures you got of the battle in the park today. Compare the crowd with the crowd in your bank pictures."

"Good idea," I said. "But can I get some interns to help? That sounds like a time consumer."

"Draft anyone you need," Robbie said. "Someone's got to stop this guy and it might as well be us."

"Couldn't agree more," I said.

Twenty minutes later I had three interns named Rich, Kelly, and Jeff sitting at computer screens trying to find the same face in a half dozen crowd scenes. I'd done an initial scan and hadn't found anything. But that didn't mean anything. This "Jewel" nutcase could be anyone.

And there were a lot of faces in those crowds.

CHECKING IN

The snow was still holding off, but the skies were getting darker and grayer when I swung down over the top of Barb Lightner's office building as Spider-Man. It was four in the afternoon and the light was on in her office, but she wasn't in there. I was about to knock on the glass when the door below opened and she came out, bundled in a long coat against the cold of the coming night.

She pulled her collar tight as she stepped onto the sidewalk and headed toward Lexington.

I jumped down off the building, landing twenty steps in front of her. "Got a minute for a friendly wall-crawler?"

Clearly I startled her and one hand instantly moved for the crease in her long coat where I would bet anything a gun was holstered. But the moment she realized it was me her hand stopped.

"You must just love scaring people with your entrances."

"Tough to ring the doorbell from the roof," I said, shrugging.

"This going to take long?"

Her eyes were cold and intense, her stance solid and almost challenging. This was one woman you didn't mess with, or waste her time.

"Nope. Just wanted to know if you've found anything on either case. And check to see how the memorial service went."

"Nothing at all on Bobbie's killer," she said, her eyes softening a little with the sentence. "And too early for the tests to come back on the radiation spot."

I nodded and let her go on.

"The service was nice. He had a lot of friends."

That sentence made her pause, then she went on.

"I've backtracked three of the zombie robbers' actions before their crimes. Possibility of a few patterns but not sure yet. Police are working the same lines, from what they're telling me."

"I'm hoping to get to the same thing," I said. "Can you use some extra help?"

"Thanks," she said, shaking her head and clearly softening a little more. "At the moment I'm better off working alone. There's something about this zombie case that has me bothered in the same way Bobbie's case does."

"You believe the zombies and Bobbie's death might be related?" I asked, trying to think of any connection I knew of. I couldn't imagine any.

"I doubt it," she said. "But you never know."

"Yeah, this is crazy enough, you do never know."

For a moment we both stood in silence, then she said, "Now before my feet freeze to the sidewalk, can I get going? I'm trying to help you here, remember."

"And I do appreciate it," I said.

I scrambled up the side of the three story brownstone and at the top glanced back. She was looking up at me.

"I'll keep in touch," I said.

"Wonderful," I think she said in return as she strode off down the street, but I couldn't be sure in the muffled sounds of the cars and the thick, cold air.

GETTING READY

After a quick stop at the *Bugle* to check on the interns' progress, I headed home for dinner. I had a sneaking suspicion, even though there had been no more robberies or shootings, that it was going to be a long night in the "city of zombies." And since I'd already been up one full night, the best thing I could do for myself was a good meal. If nothing else started up tonight, I would head back home and be in bed early, to make up for the lack of sleep last night.

Mary Jane was gone and the house was dark when I got there. I'd forgotten she had a psychology class tonight. But she'd left a note on the kitchen counter telling me how to heat up my dinner if I came home.

I wrote on the bottom of her note, "Thanks, I love you. Don't wait up." Then instead of following her directions I settled for two pieces of cold chicken and a glass of milk and ate them alone, sitting at the kitchen table.

If all those people who thought being a super hero was glamorous could see me now. Or could feel how cold my feet and hands got.

I refilled my web fluid and twenty minutes after getting home was headed back through the cold to the *Daily Bugle*. With luck, the interns would have a face for Spider-Man to find in the crowds and end this entire craziness.

But, for some reason, this case just didn't have much luck attached.

ANOTHER LONG NIGHT

The zombie robberies started off again right as the last of the massive commuter traffic was ending. I was in the *Bugle*, working with the three interns on the computers, scanning in the photos and comparing faces in the crowds, when the police radio announced a robbery in a hotel just two blocks from the *Bugle*.

"I'll see if I can get us some more pictures," I said to Jeff as I headed for the door at a run, camera in my pack over my shoulder. In the stairwell I went up instead of down, and less than five minutes later I had changed into Spider-Man, had my camera on a ledge snapping pictures of the crowd below, and had swung down the side of the hotel to a place above the main window where I could look inside.

Eight robbers, all ordinary looking people, stood with guns facing the poor hotel employees behind the long main desk. After the shoot-out in the park, there was no way I was going to wait for these people to come outside. All those employees might be dead before then.

I dropped down and moved inside the hotel through the revolving door. The warm air surrounded me like a soft glove. The silence in the large room was the most intense I had ever heard. It was as if all twenty or so employees in the room, plus the fifty or so hotel patrons were all holding their breath. Not even the sounds of the traffic penetrated that thick of silence.

One cop-for-hire held his gun on the backs of the robbers. He was short, maybe no more than five feet tall. His gun looked far too big for his hands. He had a wild, scared look in his eyes and I didn't know if I should be more worried about him shooting someone or the dead-eyed zombie robbers.

I motioned for him to put the gun down. He nodded, but didn't lower his gun much at all.

"Follow me," I said to him softly.

Again he only nodded, but did as he was told.

I moved up behind the first zombie robber on the left, a woman in a long coat and nurse's white shoes. She stood holding a gold-plated pistol on a frightened-looking man in a bad suit and red tie. His name tag read BOB.

"Excuse me," I said to the robber. No point in not being polite I always figured—especially since the woman wasn't a robber in the traditional sense. "I need to inspect this." I reached around and yanked the gun out of her hand.

She didn't resist.

I webbed her hands to the top of the check-in desk and tossed the gun to the guard.

"Don't drop it," I said to the short guy as he bumbled with the small pistol.

Behind the desk "Bob" let out a huge sigh and I thought he was going to faint right on his ugly tie.

The next gunman, an older guy with a dark beard had a much larger black gun. He also let it go easily and I repeated the procedure of webbing the robber's hands to the top of the counter and tossing the gun to the guard.

Thirty seconds later I had them all disarmed and the hotel employees and customers were giving me a round of applause as I headed out the main revolving door.

I was about to swing away when a woman about fifty paces away shouted, "Robbery!"

"Been there, done that," I said.

"Robbery," she shouted again.

I did a quick bounce off the hotel's second story and came in over the cars, people and piles of snow to where the woman was yelling.

She pointed, but I didn't need a tour guide to see what was going on. A large, fat man stood beside a cab, a gun poking inside the passenger window at the driver. The cabby was scrambling to give the guy money out of his wallet.

"Hope this guy wasn't planning on running away," I said as I dropped down beside the robber. The guy was even bigger up close. And he smelled real sour, like someone had poured milk on him six days before and he hadn't washed it off. The kind of guy you don't want to see heading toward the seat next to you on an airline. Or even on a bus for that matter.

I webbed the gun out of his thick fingers with a yank, then webbed the guy to the cab for insurance.

I turned to the woman who had screamed. "Time to call a cop," I said. I glanced back at where the huge man lay sprawled on the side of the cab roof.

I was getting more and more worried. These were ordinary people. Right now, just a few. What would happen if this "Jewel" could get a mob to act like this? What would— *could*—I do then?

BIG SOFTIE

My camera got a dozen more good pictures of the crowds in front of the bank, and I had just enough time to develop them and get them to the three blurry-eyed interns before another call came over the police scanner and I was on the run again.

Over the next few hours I stopped six zombie crimes.

Two were trying to rob theaters.

Two others were taking on cabs.

One zombie tried the cash register at a market.

The other a deli.

So far tonight none of the robbers had pulled a trigger, but I also wasn't giving them much time to even hold their guns. Better safe than sorry with this craziness.

The robbers and robberies all seemed very much the same. At midnight there hadn't been a crime called in for almost a half hour and I had managed to get pictures of three more crowds around zombie crimes. But none of my interns were left at their computer stations to do the research. Not that I blamed them. What they were doing was tedious work. I'd done it a few times myself over the years.

I got the pictures developed and left them by the computers for the three guys to work on in the morning.

I was into comparing the hotel robbery scene crowds with the deli robbery when another call came over the police scanner. There was a man with a gun walking up the middle of the road about three blocks from the *Bugle*.

"One-man zombie marching parade," I said.

By the time I could count to forty, I was swinging in over the guy, but ten counts too late. The cops had him disarmed and wrapped up. That parade was over almost before it had gotten started.

I swung up to the top of a nearby building and tucked myself in under the roof ledge to get out of the cold wind. Below me, from a height of fifty stories, the streets seemed almost normal for a winter night. Yet I knew that out there things were slowly going crazy. Someone was turning normal people into criminals. And doing it with ease.

I looked out over the huge city. There were millions of people within just a few miles of where I was. How was I going to find just one?

It seemed impossible.

I blew on my hands to warm them up, then dropped off the ledge. I'd do a short, low-level patrol around the area, then head back to the *Bugle* to work on the pictures until my eyes gave out.

Ten minutes later I swung over what seemed to be a normal city scene. A cab was stopped near the edge of the snow-filled street and a woman was beside the door, seemingly talking to the cabby. But as I got closer, the light from a nearby sign glinted off of something in the woman's hand. That wasn't a glint off of a few coins. I realized that the only conversation going on down there was with the business end of a revolver.

"Didn't anyone ever tell you," I said to the woman as I yanked the gun out of her hands with a shot of webbing, "that it was dangerous to play with guns?"

The cabby looked up at me with a huge smile of relief, then stuffed the money he had in his right hand back into his wallet. He nodded and put his cab in gear, speeding off down the street with his tires spinning.

The woman turned slowly to look at me. She seemed more like a grandmother type, with an older worn coat and good solid boots. She wasn't wearing a hat and her hair was almost silver in the dull light of the street. She reminded me of a heavier version of Aunt May.

I took her gently by the arm and led her toward the sidewalk, making sure she didn't stumble or slip on the snowdrift.

"Next time, lady," I said as we reached the sidewalk, "take the subway."

She looked up at me with puzzled eyes. Then she said, "That's where I was. How did I get out here?"

"Lady," I said, patting her shoulder, "if I knew that, this wouldn't be happening anymore. Maybe you should go home and have some nice, hot tea."

She nodded. "I think I will. Thank you for helping me out of the street. You're such a nice, young man."

"You're more than welcome," I said. She clearly didn't

remember anything else, just as the other zombie robbers didn't.

I headed up the side of the building as she turned and walked away. I watched from the top of a nearby building to make sure she did just that, disappearing down the stairs into the subway. The jails were full of enough normal people. It certainly didn't need a poor old lady gumming up the works.

I could just hear what Mary Jane would say when I told her what I'd done. She'd call me a big "softie." But she'd smile with that special smile of hers when she was saying it.

Chapter Seven
Refresh the Soul

Four A.M. Not the best time to be crawling into bed beside a wife. Especially as cold as I was.

She moaned, then rolled toward me, wrapping her warm legs and arms around me like I was the best thing she'd ever felt. Right at that moment I knew she loved me more than anything. I was icy-cold from my little toes to the tip of my hair. She didn't complain. That was true love.

She smelled good, too. That rich, sleep-smell of hers wrapped me in a warm embrace almost as well as her legs and arms.

"Thanks," I said softly into her soft hair.

"Shhhh," she said. "Sleeping."

I laid there, the luckiest man in the world, letting her body slowly warm me, while I thought back over the night. The zombie robberies had slowed down after two in the morning, as if the Jewel had gotten tired and gone to bed. I had spent an hour between three and four trying to pick a similar face out of the photos without doing anything but making my vision blur. Maybe the interns, after a fresh night's sleep, would have better luck. I sure hoped so.

I was thinking about the little old woman who robbed the cab when sleep took me.

The smell of bacon woke me from a dream of hundreds of old women pointing guns at me. All the women looked like Aunt May only with empty eyes. And they all had huge, black guns. Ugly nightmare.

I laid there and let the smell of Mary Jane's pillow and cooking bacon push the nightmare into the background. Then somehow I managed to crawl painfully into the bathroom.

After a shower I felt as if I'd actually gotten six hours of sleep instead of only four in two days. And after breakfast I was almost refreshed.

No luck, I gather?" Mary Jane asked me as I was finishing eating. She pointed at the front page of the *Bugle*.

"None," I said as I dipped up some eggs with a piece of toast. "And after that gun battle yesterday, it's getting dangerous out there."

"So nothing new on Trish's case? They let her go yesterday, but left the charges of bank robbery stand."

"Afraid she's just hooked into the overall problem. I suspect that when we find out what's behind this, all the zombie robbers will be let go with probation."

"I sure hope so."

I shrugged. "Who knows, maybe even all the charges will be dropped. There's enough real bad guys in this city to fill the jails. We don't need good people like Trish in there with them."

"That would be great if it happens that way," Mary Jane said.

"But first we got to find this *Jewel* nutcase."

I spent the next ten minutes going over all the leads and ideas from yesterday. Sometimes just talking to her made me see the missing piece.

But not this morning.

By the time I was done, it was clear she wasn't having any more luck than I was. Which meant, chances are, I hadn't found even close to all the pieces of this puzzle yet.

MORE NOTES AND LEADS

At the *Bugle*, it seemed just like every other mid-morning. One edition of the paper was put to bed, the next deadline hours away. The pace was hectic, but controlled. Most of the reporter's desks were empty. Normal morning.

But it didn't feel normal to me. I had this sense of urgency pushing me to just move a little faster.

Before seeing if the interns were having any luck, I headed

for Robbie's office. As I suspected, there was another yellow piece of paper on his desk. The *Jewel* guy liked writing notes, that much was for sure.

"Police are on their way," Robbie said, pushing the crumpled paper toward me with the end of his pencil. I turned it around with another pencil so I could read it.

Remember, I am in charge. Do not mess with my zombies.

Again it was signed: *The Jewel.*

"I sure wish he'd send them to the police instead of here," Robbie said as I finished reading and dropped down into the chair facing his desk.

"He wants the attention."

Robbie sighed. "And where better to get it than a newspaper."

"Exactly."

"My bet is pretty soon he starts making demands," I said.

"Money?"

I shrugged. "He's not getting any from his zombie robbers since no zombie has yet to escape that we know of."

"Except the ones that bring us these notes," Robbie said. "So if he doesn't need money, what could he demand?"

"Smoother streets? Horns removed from all cabs? I don't know."

Robbie laughed. "Maybe he wants to run this paper?"

"With this nutcase," I said, "anything is possible."

Behind me two uniformed police officers knocked and Robbie motioned for them to enter.

"That's my cue to get back to work," I said.

I stood and headed out the door leaving Robbie to deal with the note and the police. No doubt by now he had it down to a routine.

The three interns were huddled together around one computer as I approached.

"Got something?"

"Maybe," one intern named Rich said. He glanced at the intern named Kelly. "Show him."

Kelly's fingers moved the computer's mouse, putting two pictures side-by-side on the screen.

The third intern named Jeff leaned forward and pointed. "See the guy next to the building in the golf cap?"

"Yeah," I said.

"He's here, near that cab in this picture." Kelly pointed at the guy in the second picture.

I studied both for a moment, then nodded. "You're right. Same guy. How far apart on timing of these two pictures?" I'd taken them, but considering the last few days I couldn't remember exactly which was which.

"Different days," Rich said.

"Is he in any of the others?"

"Just found him in these two," Kelly said, smiling at me. "We'll see what we can come up with. Give us an hour."

"I'd bet anything that we find him in others," Jeff said.

Kelly laughed. "You'd bet on anything."

I stood up from staring at the computer and looked at all three. Their eyes were bright and they seemed excited. All three looked almost windblown, their faces were so red, as if they'd just walked five miles in the cold.

"One hour," I said and turned and headed into the hallway. I hated to leave them and the great lead they had found, but I knew for certain that all I'd do would be to get in their way if I stayed. Better to go check other leads and come back.

PHONING IN

I went into the darkroom and shut the door, turning on the light so anyone on the outside thought I was developing pictures and wouldn't bother me. In there I could have a little privacy. I grabbed the phone and got an outside line, then called Barb Lightner's office. She answered in one ring.

"Lightner Investigations," she said.

"Spider-Man here," I said, glancing around to make sure the door behind me was still closed.

"You can use a phone?" Barb said. "I am impressed."

"A fellow can't win with you," I said. "Complain if I drop by, sarcasm if I phone. You must be hell on dates."

She laughed. "Wouldn't know. No one dares ask me out."

"So," I said quickly, making sure I didn't start down that road with her dead husband. "Any leads?"

"Still piling stuff up," she said. "But I might have a few. From the looks of this morning's paper, I've got as many as the police. You got a few minutes to meet me for an interview with two of the zombie robbers? They were kicked loose this morning and agreed to talk with me to try to help."

"Where and when?"

"Ten minutes," she said. "Deli on the corner two blocks east of my office."

"I'll be the guy in the red suit," I said.

"What? No flower on the lapel?"

Before I could snap a comeback, she'd hung up. Man, she was good.

ZOMBIES TALK

I was still warm and toasty from the good night's sleep and the solid breakfast, but too much swinging between the buildings today was going to take away that heat quickly. Cold didn't describe the day.

Bitter was more like it.

One of those days a person wished it would snow because that would mean it had warmed up.

I tucked myself under a roof ledge in some shadows, positioned so I could see the corner Barb had indicated. Franklin's Deli didn't look busy, but it was still early. By lunch I would bet it was packed.

Barb, wearing the same long coat as yesterday, reached the

corner and looked around. She was a striking woman even from a distance.

She stood there, pacing for a moment, then waved as two women moved toward her along the sidewalk. I remembered them from the night before. Both had tried to rob different theater box offices. Wow, the police were springing the zombie robbers fast. Talk about revolving-door jail cells. With this weird crime wave, that term applied.

I let Barb talk to them a moment. I could tell at the exact second when she told them I would be joining them. Both looked startled and glanced up and around. A wave was tempting, but I resisted.

I waited for them to go back to talking directly to Barb before I dropped off the ledge and swung down onto the sidewalk behind them.

"Excuse me, ladies," I said. "Mind if I join you?"

One woman, a young-looking bank clerk type swallowed and said, "No problem."

I could tell that the other woman wasn't so sure, but didn't say no. She was older, maybe early sixties, with silver hair and dark eyes. She wore a long, expensive coat and thick leather gloves.

"This is Carmen," Barb said, indicating the younger woman. "And this is Betty."

I bowed slightly, first to the older woman named Betty, then Carmen. "I'm pleased the police have released you."

I opened the deli door for them and held it.

"A gentleman super hero," Barb said. "Wonders will never cease."

"I just need the white horse and the armor," I said.

"Better than spandex and a bug-eyed mask," Barb said, smiling at me as she went past.

"Ouch," I said.

Both women seemed stunned at the exchange, so I said nothing more until we were seated in a booth hidden from the view of the street. It felt odd to be sitting inside a restaurant in my Spider-Man clothes. It didn't happen often. In fact, I couldn't remember the last time.

At least it was warmer than a rooftop.

Barb slid in first and I sat beside her, leaving the other two women to sit facing us.

A skinny waitress with a stained apron came up and sort of snorted at me. "Nice suit. Can't get enough of Halloween, huh?"

"Actually, I'm Spider-Man's biggest fan."

Barb patted my arm. "Don't mind my friend here. Tough childhood."

The waitress again snorted and just walked away. My guess was this deli just became self-serve for us.

Barb smiled at the two women, ignoring the waitress. "Thanks for talking to us."

"Yes, thank you," I said. "The city needs all the help it can get on this insanity."

Both women nodded, then Carmen said, "I'm not sure what we can tell you that we haven't already told the police."

"You never know," Barb said. "We may be able to put your information together with other information we have to help the police."

Again both woman nodded as if their heads were tied to the same string.

I started the questions after a short moment of strained silence. "Do either of you remember me stopping your robbery last night?"

"No," the older woman said.

"I remember coming to," Carmen said, "sort of like waking up, and you were there with my purse gun wrapped in your spider-webbing."

"Did you feel numb at all?" Barb asked.

"No," Carmen said. "It was just suddenly I was aware. But I had no idea how I got to where I was."

"Same for me," Betty said.

"At first I thought you had taken my gun and I was about to

get angry," Carmen said. "But then it came clear I had tried to rob the theater box office and you had stopped me."

"You remember doing it?" I asked.

"Oh, not at all," Carmen said. "It was just clear from everything around me. And how you were holding me until the cop handcuffed me."

I nodded. "Hope I didn't hurt you."

She smiled. "Oh, you didn't. You were very gentle."

"All the ladies say that," I said.

Betty actually smiled at my lame joke while Carmen giggled.

"So what is the last thing you remember before that?" Barb asked.

"Being on the subway," Carmen said.

"You also?" I asked Betty. "On the subway?"

"Yes, sir," Betty said. "I told the police there was this man with sunglasses and a baseball cap who sat down next to me. Only his cap wasn't a baseball team. It said, SANDPINES or something like that."

"Sandpines?" Barb said. "Weird."

I glanced at Barb, but I hadn't told her about the intern's discovery of the man in the photos yet and didn't want to in front of the women.

"You remember a man dressed like that on your subway?" Barb asked Carmen.

"Honestly," Carmen said, "I wasn't paying any attention at all to anyone on the train. Long day, new book. You know how it is."

"Yeah," Barb said, "actually I do."

I said nothing. I doubt these woman needed the idea in their minds that Spider-Man rode a subway.

For the next fifteen minutes both Barb and I asked the two women all the questions we could think of. There was really nothing new beyond the man in the strange cap and both women's memories stopping on the subway.

And we never did get served.

We walked the two out to the sidewalk and thanked them again. Then I walked with Barb toward her office.

"If I had a bet," I said, "it would be that the Jewel recruited his zombies somehow on the subways."

"I agree," Barb said. "But we don't know for sure yet."

She then told me she had two other zombie robbers to interview this afternoon.

"You want me along?" I asked, stopping in front of her office.

"Are you kidding?" she said, laughing. "You almost gave old Betty a heart attack back there."

"I'm not that scary."

"Not to me," Barb said. "That's true."

She patted me on the arm and headed up the sidewalk, leaving me struggling for a good comeback line again. Why was it she had that affect on me?

"Stop by after five," she said with her back to me as she opened her front door. "I'll have more information. You bring the pictures."

"Yes, ma'm," I said, in a stern military voice.

"Don't forget to salute," she said without ever looking back at me.

The front door closed long before I even realized she had gotten me again.

Chapter Eight
Charts and Facts

By the time I got back to the *Bugle,* the three interns had found a couple more pictures with the guy in the golf cap hanging out in the crowds of robberies. This guy was either in the wrong place at the wrong time a great deal, or our Jewel guy. Problem was none of the pictures were clear enough shots of the guy's face to get an identification.

The interns, excited at what they had found, went back to work scanning more photos while I stopped by Robbie's office to tell him about the progress.

Robbie was impressed. "Keep them at it." Then he shoved a sheet of paper across his desk at me. "Take a look at this."

The sheet was filled with a list of names down the left side with the header over the column "Zombies." At first glance I could tell it was some of the zombie robbers, including Mary Jane's friend Trish Mathews.

Across the top of the paper were three more column headers. First column was titled "Location of Robbery." Second was "Target of Robbery" and third was "Location of Last Memory." Across from each name the information had been typed in.

"We've talked to twenty of the zombies," Robbie said. "And added the information we got from the police to ours. Interesting, huh?"

Interesting didn't begin to describe this chart. All the zombie last memories were on or near a subway. Just as Barb had suspected.

"Police have this?" I asked.

"They do," he said. "And we're not printing it yet, either. No point in telling this nutcase we're gaining on him."

"So true," I said. "This nails where he finds his victims."

"That it does," Robbie said. "But the location of the robberies I find even more interesting."

I scanned down the column until I finally saw the pattern. All the robberies had occurred in a fairly small area of about six by ten city blocks. "You got a map?"

"Setting up a war room," Robbie said. "Map and all. Two interns should have it ready, robbery locations pinned on the map and all by later this afternoon."

"Great," I said, jumping up and heading for the door.

"You got an idea?"

I shrugged. "If he's working in this tight an area, I might be able to get more pictures for us." I didn't tell Robbie that as Spider-Man patrolling those blocks, I also might stop some of the crimes before they happened. Or maybe even see the guy in the cap. It was a long shot, but worth the time.

"Go for it," Robbie said. "Just be careful on the subways. I don't want to be bailing you out of jail."

That thought actually made me shudder.

THE FIRST TO DIE

Outside, the snow was starting to fall again, swirling on a slight wind, not sticking to the ground, but filling the air over the streets and making it dark enough that many streetlights had come on even though it was an hour before official sundown.

To see anyone clearly on the sidewalks below, I needed to be fairly low. I set up a pattern of moving along the walls of buildings near the third floor level, stopping and spending a few extra minutes on the corners where there were subway entrances.

Since it was snowing, almost no one looked up and saw me. Everyone walked, head down, collars up, hats pulled low. It was that kind of day. I wished I could do the same thing.

It took me about an hour to cover most of the area of the robberies.

Nothing.

Not a sign of the guy in the weird hat.

And thankfully no zombie robberies.

But I was frozen solid.

I headed back to the *Bugle* and put on my regular clothes. After a cup of coffee and ten minutes standing in front of a small space heater a reporter had brought in, I was thawed enough to go back out. I grabbed copies of the four photos that had the man in the golf hat in them, plus a copy of Robbie's chart, then somehow managed to get back into my wet and cold Spider-Man costume. Putting on a wet, cold swimming suit is bad enough. This was worse.

A full body-length worse.

Barb was in her office when I knocked on the window.

Without even turning she shouted, "It's open." She was getting used to me coming and going it seemed.

I slid the window up and dropped in beside her, pulling the heavy glass closed behind me before too much of the swirling snow could fill the air.

"Four shots," I said, not waiting for the pleasantries as I tossed the photos on her desk in front of her.

I stood beside her for a long thirty seconds while she studied them in silence, then I tossed the chart on top of the photos. "Amazing," she said after a moment of staring at it. "All subway origins as we figured. And all the robberies in a relatively small area. Where did you get these?"

"I have my sources, just like you. Let's leave it at that."

She stared at me for a moment, then smiled a small, knowing smile and nodded. "What else?" she asked.

"I patrolled that area this afternoon for an hour," I said. "Sixty square blocks is not that small, trust me. I'm headed back out there now."

I started for the window.

"I'll roam the subway platforms in that area," she said. "See if I can spot this weird cap the guy seems to like to wear."

"You don't need to do that, you know," I said.

"Yes I do," she said, turning and for the first time looking up at me. "Bobby was murdered right in the middle of that area the night before this all started."

"I can't imagine how it could be connected," I said. And I couldn't. Nothing at all seemed to link the two crimes except the area and the timing.

"Neither can I," Barb said, her voice soft. "But if it is . . ."

I nodded. "You've got to be there."

"Right," she said. She turned back to stare at the pictures. Or more likely, lost in the pictures of Bobby's body that haunted her mind.

"Make sure you call for backup if you spot the guy. I'll stay close to police scanners when I can."

She nodded. "I will."

"Promise?"

"Scout's honor and all that," she said, still not looking up.

I left her staring at the pictures and went back out the window into the cold night air.

At that moment seven blocks away an elderly woman walked stiffly up to the counter of a deli and stuck a gun in the cashier's face.

The cashier ducked behind the counter in a panic, grabbed the owner's loaded gun from below the cash register, and came up firing. It happened so fast the grandmother didn't even have a chance to snap out of the trance and wonder how she got into the deli.

Things had suddenly changed.

The first zombie robber had died.

And I had no doubt she wouldn't be the last.

A LONG, SAD NIGHT

That night I stopped six zombie robberies and helped in the capture of ten other zombies, all by two in the morning.

I alternated between patrolling the sides of the buildings over the streets, standing next to cop cars listening to the police scanners, and warming up at the *Bugle* next to the police scanner there.

During the long evening I saw Barb twice on the sidewalk, but didn't talk to her.

The entire night had a dead feel, as if the snow dampened every sound down. After a few hours it almost felt as if the city itself was mourning for that poor grandmother. I had gotten to the scene just in time to see them take her body away. It made me angry and even more determined.

And also very sad.

By four in the morning I was in the "Jewel" war room, adding pins to the big map that filled one wall. Again all the zombie robberies were in the same sixty square block area.

On the map of the city the area seemed small. And the farther I stood from the map, the smaller it looked. But I knew after working those blocks all night just how large it really was.

Too large.

IT NEVER ENDS

The zombie robberies started earlier the next afternoon, with six men holding up a bank while five other women went into a second bank two blocks away. This Jewel nut was getting creative with the sexes. Or just making sure we all knew he was in control of the zombies in some way or another. He didn't need to convince me of that point any more.

This time all the robbers moved quicker, as if they were actually trying to get away.

None of them did.

But it was odd to see them try.

When they came out of the bank all the robbers scattered, as if they all had just made a normal bank stop and had places to go with their ill-taken money. They didn't run or act scared. They just simply went in different directions.

Did them no good at all. I got them all easily.

That afternoon the interns found two more pictures from

different robberies with the guy in his weird golf hat standing in the crowd. Still no clear picture of his face.

At the men's bank hold-up I scanned the crowd for the guy, but didn't see him. I took some pictures just to be sure. My luck he had been watching the other bank job.

That night I stopped twelve other robberies and missed ten more between getting warmed up and out of touch of the police scanners.

Somehow this Jewel guy was increasing the pace, getting more daring, more creative. That wasn't a good sign at all. Didn't he know that too much creativity could be dangerous?

By three in the morning it all seemed to grind to a halt. Both the robberies and the snow seemed to stop at the same time and the streets of the city again seemed relatively safe under a layer of fresh whiteness.

I again spent an hour in the "Jewel war room" adding pins to the map. It was getting to be one cluttered map. Not one pin was outside the sixty block area.

On the way home I went back over the day. The only good thing that had happened was that no one was killed and I had managed to get six more photos of robbery gawkers on the intern's desk for work in the morning.

Barb had spent the late afternoon and most of the evening again walking the subway platforms in the area, also without luck. I didn't talk to her, but she nodded to me once.

All around, just a bad day.

LEAVE THE GUNS AT HOME!

The next morning the *Bugle* headlines and TV and radio reports warned people who carried registered guns to leave them at home or bring them to police stations for temporary storage until the crisis was over. It seemed the police had found another similarity among the zombies that had been so obvious I hadn't even thought of it.

Robbie admitted he hadn't either.

All the zombies carried and used their own guns. The Jewel was only targeting people who were already armed. Neither Robbie, or Barb, or I had any idea how he managed that. How could he know who had a gun in a purse and who didn't? That just didn't seem possible. But making people rob places against their will also didn't seem possible. The only bad thing was that we weren't sure if the people with unregistered guns would do the smart thing and keep their weapons at home, too—or if the Jewel knew about those people as well.

The Jewel was getting more frightening by the minute.

None of the photos I had taken the night before had the guy in the strange hat in the crowd as far as the interns could find. At least that showed that I hadn't missed him. That would have made me really mad, and considering how short my temper was getting from lack of sleep, getting mad wasn't a good idea.

As the day before, the robberies started near three in the afternoon, with zombies seeming to appear everywhere. The same two banks as yesterday were hit again, this time by three zombies each.

I was starting to feel sorry for those bank tellers. Maybe the bank should give them hazard pay. Or combat pay. I doubt many soldiers had had as many guns pointed at them as some of those tellers.

Barb and I talked twice during the afternoon about possible leads, but neither of us really had anything.

The snow held off, but nothing warmed up.

I spent all afternoon and evening chasing down zombie robbers. The same as I had done yesterday.

And the day before that.

Barb spent her afternoon and evening walking the subway platforms along with dozens of undercover cops, all hoping to catch the guy.

Just as she had done yesterday.

And the day before that.

All for nothing.

Just a big, flat zero.

At four in the morning I poked the pins into the map in the war room and headed for home, disgusted and completely exhausted. This nightmare was never going to end, I was sure.

Mary Jane tucked me in with the promise to wake me in three hours. My last thought as I drifted off was to wonder how things could get worse.

Sometimes I could be so blasted short-sighted.

THINGS CAN GET WORSE

On day seven of the zombie robberies things took a very ugly turn in a very wrong direction. It started as I dragged my tired body into the news room just after ten. Two cops were standing in Robbie's office, working over something. I waited until they were finished, then went in.

"Another note?"

Robbie nodded and dropped down into his chair. He had a look of disgust and anger on his face.

"What's the nutcase want this time?"

"Nothing," Robbie said, "as always. Just more threats."

"What kind of threats?"

"The note said that because the police and Spider-Man hadn't left his zombies alone as he told us to, people would start dying this afternoon."

The thought of zombies killing just plain made me sick. The grandmother had been the only death. And except for the gun battle in the park where no one was hit, the zombies so far had only been interested in robbing people and businesses. But after watching that gun battle, I had no doubt the Jewel was capable of getting normal people to kill for him.

And there would be no telling who or where a completely normal person would stop, pull out a gun and start firing. It wouldn't be possible for me to even stop a tenth of those. And unless people obeyed the police's order not to carry guns, that meant a lot of innocent people on both sides of the gun were going to be killed.

"I hope he has second thoughts," I said to Robbie. "No one's going to be able to stop all of it."

"Yeah," Robbie said softly, staring at his ceiling. "I know."

PHOTO HELP

Of the three interns working on the photos, Jeff had been brought on board at the *Bugle* for his photo skills. When I stopped by to check on their progress after leaving Robbie's office, they were in the process of hatching a plot on their own. I knew their thinking instantly from all the camera equipment scattered on the table.

I picked up a camera and studied it for a moment before glancing first at Richard, then Kelly, and finally Jeff.

"Look, Peter," Jeff said. "We're not finding anything in the photos we have. We need more pictures. Better pictures of the crowds."

"True," I said. "We do need more pictures. And you three think you're going to go out and get them? Right?"

All three nodded.

Then Jeff said, "Four of us roaming the streets instead of just you should get us a few more pictures, if the robberies continue."

"It also might get you three killed," I said. "Ever seen what a bullet can do to you?"

At that instant the image of Bobby's body flashed into my mind. In a sense, he had been Barb's intern. One bullet had made a very large hole in his head. There was no chance in the world these three were hitting the streets.

"We're adults," Kelly said. "We can take care of ourselves."

"You're also interns," I said. "And I doubt the paper's insurance would cover this little idea of yours."

Richard looked at me. "Afraid for your job? Jeff here is pretty darn good."

I just shook my head. Richard had guts, and he *was* good with a camera, but on a case like this, you needed experience.

"Tell you what," I said. "Let's have Robbie make the call. He says you can go out on the streets with cameras for the *Bugle,* it's fine by me."

All three sort of half-nodded.

Ten minutes later Robbie had set them very straight and all three were back going over photos again, safely tucked in their room with their computers. It seemed that all three very much wanted to continue being interns at the paper.

HE'S BACK!

I took to the streets in the sixty block area early. The sky was gray and the temperature was holding just above twenty degrees. About every thirty minutes the wind would swirl between the buildings a little and a light dusting of snow would fill the air. I couldn't tell if it was new snow, or just the wind blowing last night's snow off the roofs and ledges of the buildings.

At about ten minutes until three I was crouched on a third-story building ledge just above a patrol car. The heavy-set cop in the car was named Stan and he'd helped me a couple times over the past few nights get to and stop robberies. He knew I was up here. So at the moment I had the best setup I could think of. I was high enough to see blocks in three directions and two subway entrances, plus close to a police scanner.

Every time a guy came out of the subway stairs wearing a baseball-like cap, I half jerked. And until the last few days I hadn't realized how many thousands of men wore those baseball/golf hats. They seemed to be everywhere.

This morning Mary Jane had woken me out of a nightmare where I was buried by the stupid caps and couldn't climb out. All of them said "Sandpines" on the front.

Another in a series of very ugly dreams. I doubt the nightmares were going to stop until this was over. Of course, I doubted I was going to get much sleep until this was over anyway, so what did it matter.

Below me the cop's car door shoved open and Stan stuck his head out and looked up at me. "Robbery going down two blocks south off Broadway. Bank on the corner."

"Thanks!" I shouted at him as I shot a web at the building across the street and jumped into the air. I doubt he heard me, since he had slammed his car door shut and was horsing his patrol car out into traffic right behind me.

Weird. This was the first one outside of the sixty square block area. Had the Jewel expanded his stomping grounds? I sure hoped not.

At the bank I expected to see what I had been seeing over the last seven days: regular people standing stiffly holding guns on scared tellers. But not this time.

I swung in over the bank just as a guy dressed in a bright red and white striped costume and wearing a striped hood emerged from the bank holding a very strange-looking red and white rifle.

"You have got to be kidding me?" I said out loud.

The Candy-Man was back.

The Candy-Man, as he called himself, was a stupid, two-bit crook who dressed up like a giant lollipop and used a gun that shot hardened candies at his victims. I had put him away before and seeing him now didn't help my bad mood in the slightest. I had enough real problems with this Jewel and his zombies without losers like the Candy-Man coming back now.

"When did they let you out of the loony bin?" I asked, landing on the wall over the striped idiot.

He spun around and looked up, barely keeping his feet on the slick sidewalk. If a candy cane could look afraid, this one did. "Spider-Man . . . you . . . you can't stop me."

"A stuttering lollipop," I said. "Next thing you know we'll have burping candy bars. Then growling gummies. Oh, where will it all stop?"

My spider-sense warned me of danger as he pulled up his gun and fired. I guess my poking fun at him had made him mad.

Bummer.

I jumped sideways and over him.

Hard candy shattered against the brick wall where I had been, smashing into powder.

"You know that stuff gives you bad teeth," I said as I landed behind him.

He spun around and I knocked him down and wrapped him up with webbing before he knew what hit him.

It felt so good.

It would have felt better if it had been the Jewel.

He went tumbling backward, ending up against the side of the building, his candy-suit cocooned in webbing and snow.

The guy went down quicker than anyone I had ever seen before. "Oh, come on," I said. "I didn't hit you that hard. I was saving my best stuff."

Stan and two other patrol cars slid to a stop behind me while I stood over the dazed Candy-Man.

"No zombie?" Stan asked as he came up beside me.

"Just an idiot with a candy jaw," I said. "But be careful. He may be sticky."

Stan glanced at the wrapped up Candy-Man, then at me, then he laughed.

It sounded really, really nice.

Chapter Nine
A New Door

Day eight started with two hours of nightmarish sleep and a shower. Now I sat at the breakfast table, slumped over like a worm hanging on a fisherman's hook, feeling just about as good. Not even the wonderful smells of bacon and coffee that filled the kitchen helped. I needed about two days of sleep. Fat chance of that happening anytime soon. Until this Jewel guy was caught, I wasn't going to get much sleep at all.

I had promised Mary Jane I would come home for breakfast every day, if nothing else. I had managed over the last seven nights an average of three hours of sleep, plus breakfast. I was glad now I had done that. On the street things were getting worse. Even with all the leads, it didn't seem as if we were any closer to getting this nutcase. I needed a little rest each day to give my body a chance to recharge. At the moment it didn't feel like it was recharging. More like it was being punished.

Mary Jane poured the batter for two pancakes onto the grill and then moved over behind me to rub my shoulders. "From the looks of the paper it wasn't pretty out there last night."

"It got uglier as the night went on," I said, my head sideways on the table top. "Six dead, ten wounded. All innocent people."

"Oh," Mary Jane said softly and stopped rubbing my shoulders. She moved silently back over to the pancakes and flipped them over.

The silence filled the kitchen, broken only by the sizzling from the stove. There just wasn't anything I could say about all those people getting hurt. I had stopped a lot more from getting hurt, but I hadn't been able to stop it all. And now I just didn't want to think about it.

Somehow this Jewel nutcase could find out if a person had

a gun on them, get them to disobey the police, and send them to rob and/or shoot others.

How Jewel was doing that I had no idea. And how he figured out who had the guns and who didn't I couldn't figure out either. No one could. I was starting to believe that every person in the city carried guns.

But with luck, the people would listen to the paper and the police and leave the guns at home.

Mary Jane put the wonderful-smelling pancakes on a plate, nudged me into an upright position, and slid them in front of me. "Eat what you can," she said. "It'll help you feel better."

"What would make me feel better is if about seven million people just stayed home today so our Jewel nutcase would stand out like an ugly thumb."

She moved around and again started rubbing my shoulders. "Well, I've canceled my appointments today," she said. "And some studying I need to do for class."

"Thanks," I said. "One less thing for me to worry about."

"Just promise me again you'll come home for at least breakfast, no matter how bad things get."

"Promise," I said. "And maybe even a little sleep as long as you don't mind the cold feet in bed."

"Actually," she said, kissing the top of my head, "I look forward to them."

I let the little white lie stand. I had no doubt it was going to be the nicest thing anyone would say to me all day.

MORE CHARTS, MORE SLEEP

First stop on the way to the *Bugle* was Barb's office. I'd seen her last night at ten and told her I'd stop by at nine to compare notes. She was sitting at her desk, back to the window, head on her left hand.

I slid the window up after a quick knock and dropped in beside her. Clearly she hadn't spent any time at home last night. She had on the same clothes as yesterday and her hair looked as if her fingers had been her only comb.

"Take a look at the chart," she said, pointing to the wall next to the door.

I did as she said, moving around in front of the desk.

Impressive work. She had taken the list of zombie robbers I'd given her, then added twice as many names of robbers that she had talked to, or got information from her police sources. Each robber had a small mark beside the name showing where the information had come from.

As with my list, she'd broken down the chart into three categories.

Last remembered location on all of them was the subway. That cinched that fact solidly.

But then she'd gone even further by taking the last remembered location and grouping them into areas.

She had also grouped the location of all the crimes into areas. And out of that organization had come some more facts.

"The guy likes four subway stations," I said aloud. "Amazing. Man is that going to narrow the search some."

"Seems that way," Barb said from behind me. "He might also like the trains between those four stations."

"Police have this?"

"An hour ago," she said. "I gave it to Hawkins. He's going to focus all the police energy on those lines and stations."

"Nice work," I said, turning back to face her. I was half-stunned at what I saw. I thought I felt bad, but I didn't feel half as bad as she looked. Huge dark circles were under her eyes, and she looked as pale as the snow on the ledge outside the window. What with Bobby getting killed and then this, her reserves were gone.

"Thanks," she said, her voice rough.

"Now it's time for some rest," I said, moving around the desk and helping her out of her chair even though she half resisted.

"Can't," she said. "Too much to do."

"And it will still be waiting to do in a few hours."

"What are you? A doctor?"

"A doctor in a spider suit. Yeah, I can see that working."

She only grunted.

I led her by the arm to the couch and pushed her down. Her resistance was half-hearted at best. I knew, without a doubt that if she wanted to fight, she could. And would.

I waited until she stretched out, then took a blanket folded on the back of the couch and covered her.

"Maybe just a few minutes," she said, turning on her side and closing her eyes.

"Make it a few hours and you got yourself a deal," I said.

She half-smiled at me, eyes still closed.

By the time I got out the window she was asleep. It was the first time I'd gotten away from her with the last word.

STRANGE MESSENGER BOY

At the *Bugle,* I stopped in the photo room first. Interns Kelly, Rich, and Jeff had managed to find six more times that the man in the strange Sandpines golf cap was in the crowd of a robbery. One of the enlarged pictures gave a pretty decent side view of the guy's face. I didn't recognize him and I would have if I knew him, considering his large, down-turned nose and thick eyebrows. He had what is called a "distinctive face."

I'd sure recognize him now.

In all the photos, no matter what day, he wore a brown flight jacket, the golf hat with Sandpines scripted across the top, and jeans. Guy didn't change clothes much. I only hoped he didn't start now.

"Great job," I said to the guys. "Robbie seen this?"

"A half hour ago," Jeff said. "Police have copies, too."

"You guys just may have helped stop this insanity," I said,

turning for the door to the newsroom. I just hoped my words weren't premature. So far nothing about this had been easy.

The first words out of Robbie's mouth as I went into his office were, "Seen the picture?"

"Just did."

"Recognize him?"

"Nope. But having the picture should help."

"We can only hope," Robbie said, "after last night."

All morning I had been doing my best to not think about last night and all the innocent people in zombie state shooting and killing other innocent people. Unless the police or I had some luck today, more people were going to die.

"Yeah," I said. Then I changed the subject. "Police also have a better sense of the Jewel's main subway haunts."

"How?" Robbie asked, sitting forward and staring at me.

I dropped down into the chair facing his desk. "I gave the chart you made yesterday to Spider-Man. Spider-Man is working with an ex-cop, private detective named Barb Lightner on a case she thinks might be related."

"Is it?" Robbie asked.

"No way of knowing," I said. "Her assistant got murdered in an alley the night before all this started. She thinks it might be. Sort of a gut-hunch."

Robbie nodded. "Yeah, I remember that murder. Weird one with the melted spot in the snow."

"That's the one," I said. "Spider-Man gave her your list and she had another of her own, plus information from the police. She put them all together to get the Jewel's favorite subway haunts. With the photo, the police ought to have a decent shot at him today. More than any other day."

"Could we be that lucky?" Robbie asked.

"More innocent people are going to die if someone doesn't get lucky soon."

"You have that right."

Suddenly, my spider-sense buzzed. Robbie was looking over my shoulder at something going on in the newsroom.

Then his eyes narrowed and he got a very, very cold expression on his face.

I spun around as Robbie grabbed the phone. What I saw was a jaw-dropper.

Hank "The Animal" Hancock stood in the center of the newsroom, facing me, not moving. He wore a long, fur-collared coat and a fur-lined hat. If I didn't know him, I would have thought the guy was a prominent millionaire just from his appearance instead of a man who was known for killing someone just for asking a stupid question.

"Get the police to the newsroom. Quick!" Robbie said into the phone.

In the newsroom three reporters inched up from their computers and slowly backed away from Hancock. I didn't blame them. Chances are that under that coat Hancock carried at least half a dozen weapons. And he was known for being willing to use them at any time, for almost any stupid little reason.

He was probably the city's most wanted non-super-villian criminal. He ran a syndicate of petty thieves, bookies, and prostitution rings with an iron hand. As far as anyone knew, he hadn't been seen in public for almost a year. And because he was so insulated by layers of front men, no one seemed to know where he actually lived, or if he was even in the city at any given time.

As Spider-Man, I had gone looking for him a few times after one crime or another. But just as with the police, I had never been able to find him. Now he had just walked into the *Bugle* newsroom and was standing, staring at me and Robbie.

"Wonder what he wants?" I said, standing and moving toward the glass door.

"Why don't we wait for the police to find out," Robbie said.

"If he waits that long," I said. As I got closer to the door I could see Hancock's eyes. In them was a look I had seen far too many times over the last few days.

Deadness.

Nothing.

No one home.

"He's a zombie," I said.

"You're kidding," Robbie said, moving up beside me and staring at him. "You're not kidding. For heaven's sake, don't startle him awake."

"Not planning to," I said. "But after last night I'm not sure which way he's the most dangerous."

"Good point," Robbie said.

We both stood silently, watching Hancock stare at us with his dead eyes.

The newsroom emptied slowly as people tiptoed out the doors as if not wanting to wake a sleeping monster.

The city's most wanted criminal stood silent and still, controlled by the Jewel's zombie instructions.

Whatever those instructions were.

Was he going to open fire?

Or just stand there?

There was no telling.

The minutes dragged by.

Or maybe it was just seconds. I had no way of judging. Nothing around me was moving, and I couldn't see a newsroom clock from where I stood.

Finally the intercom on Robbie's desk broke into life.

"Police on the way up."

"About time," Robbie said to himself.

A few moments later the door on the far side of the newsroom opened slowly and Sergeants Hawkins and Drew crawled through, one moving left, the other right.

Hancock stared at me with his zombie eyes.

The two cops took their time.

I didn't move.

Robbie didn't move.

Hancock didn't move.

Seconds lasting minutes ticked past.

Finally the two sergeants were in position. With a nod to me and Robbie, they jumped out from behind desks and grabbed each of Hancock's arms, making sure he couldn't move.

The moment they reached Hancock, I went through the door. "Careful," I said. "He may have a bomb under that coat."

Drew nodded and eased open Hancock's coat. Nothing under it that I could see except a very expensive suit.

They locked his hand behind his back and then were careful as they frisked Hancock.

Very careful.

Robbie and I watched.

They found three different guns. And a note on yellow legal paper.

"Another note from the Jewel," Robbie said, using a handkerchief to carefully open the paper.

"Nice choice of delivery boys," I said as Drew slapped a second set of handcuffs roughly on Hancock. They were taking no chances with this guy and I liked that idea.

Suddenly the criminal's eyes were full of life again.

I ducked back into Robbie's office and got my camera, then came back out as Hancock was gaining his senses.

"What? Where am I?" he asked, glancing around. "How did I get here? What is the meaning of this?" He was one very confused crook. And I could tell he was slowly getting very, very angry.

"Seems someone wants your job," I said to him. "Bummer, huh? Now smile?"

I clicked two quick photos.

"Ever hear of a guy named Jewel?" Robbie asked.

"The scum who's messing up my businesses," Hancock said, almost spitting. "If I ever find him, I'll kill him."

"Seems as if he found you first," I said, clicking a few more pictures.

Hancock glanced at Drew, then at the newsroom, seeming to realize completely, for the first time, where he was. And what had happened to him.

Then he looked back at me. He had this look in his eyes that I would call something between poison and pure evil. I'd seen it a number of times over the years in the eyes of those I had fought. The Green Goblin. Carnage. They all had the same look in their eyes. It always made me shudder. This morning was no exception.

But I still took the picture. With luck, it would capture the look in the eyes.

"And now you're all ours," Drew said, yanking Hancock toward the door and into the arms of two more cops waiting there.

I watched him go for a moment, then turned back to read the note over Robbie and Sergeant Hawkins's shoulders.

> *I am tired of playing small games with the sheep-like people of this city. Starting today I will form a new criminal underworld, with me at the top. My zombies will control all crime, all police, all the city government. Do not try to stop me.*

It was signed *The Jewel.*

"Guy has a real ego," I said.

"Seems his messenger proves he can do the deed," Robbie said.

"I haven't doubted he could in days," I said. "I just hope all those cops watching those subway stations realize the same thing today. You might want to warn them that if he can control Hancock, he can control cops with guns."

Sergeant Hawkins looked up at me with a clearly shocked look on his face. I could tell that was something he hadn't thought about before. Another of those "too obvious" facts.

To be honest, until I saw what the Jewel had done to Hancock, I hadn't thought of it either. Maybe it had been lucky that I hadn't seen the guy over the last few nights. No telling at all what he could have done with Spider-Man.

But yet someone had to stop the *Jewel.* The question now was how?

Chapter Ten
Joining Forces

The snow was back by noon, drifting between the buildings, swirling in the wakes of the cabs, covering the streets. The radio stations and the television stations were all repeating over and over that everyone should leave their guns at home, licensed or not. It was becoming like a mantra around the city.

I had spent most of the late morning patrolling the areas above the Jewel's favorite subway stations, hoping to get lucky and see that distinctive hat and hooked nose walking the streets. All I had gotten for my effort was chilled to the bone. So when the snow started falling, I decided a little heat was needed.

Besides that, I still wasn't sure what I would do if I did see the guy. More than likely come in behind him and knock him out. Take no chances of becoming a zombie.

I was standing beside the police scanner, holding my hands over a small heater in the newsroom when another bank robbery started. "Shots fired," the dispatcher said.

Those two words were the last words I wanted to hear.

The bank being robbed was my bank, the same one that had been hit when I was in line the first day, the same one that had been robbed seven times over the last few days. After a teller had been shot yesterday, the bank's management had gotten angry and brought in a small hired police force. It was going to be a blood bath if I didn't get there soon.

It took me fifteen seconds to get to the roof and ten more seconds to change clothes. Another fifteen seconds to get through the falling snow to the bank. That was as fast as I had moved in a long, long time.

The scene was like a bad western movie.

Outside the bank, people scrambled for cover or gawked from nearby windows. Inside the bank was another matter.

Two bank guards were down, bleeding on the marble floor. One zombie robber, a woman in a nurse's uniform, was also shot and leaning against a pillar looking shocked, holding her shoulder with a bloody hand.

The rest of the bank guards were on their stomachs, hands over their heads, being guarded by a zombie robber. A new development. The robbers had never worked together like that before. And how they had managed to out-gun those guards was beyond me.

Eight other zombie robbers were headed for the front door of the bank, all carrying bags and sacks which I assumed were filled with money. They came out together, pouring out the front door and onto the sidewalk like a mass of ants. The instant they hit the street they all started shooting, scattering in both directions as they fired and fired.

I swung down through the middle of them, my spider-sense going wild as I yanked guns out of two of the robber's hands. "Zombies aren't allowed to play with guns," I said.

Both ignored me and my humor and just kept running in different directions. For the moment, I let them go. At least they were now unarmed.

Two other zombie robbers took up positions behind a car and started firing at the three police cars that flanked the bank front. The police returned fire, breaking out the car's windows.

Sounds of the shots seemed muffled in the snow.

Bullets thumped into cars and snow banks.

One bullet smashed a window in a deli and sent those inside scrambling for cover.

My spider-sense warned me to jump just as a zombie woman in a red coat and stocking cap took a shot at my back. I did a quick kick off the wall and fired webbing at her gun, putting it out of action.

My spider-sense went wild again as bullets snapped into the snow bank in front of me. I spun around to face a man in a leather jacket pointing a very nasty-looking pistol at my stomach.

Before he could get off another shot I covered the gun and his hand with a ball of webbing, then yanked.

The man went face first into a snowbank. I wrapped his legs in webbing just to make sure he stayed put.

As for the two shooters behind the car, I did a handspring over the hood of the car and webbed their arms to their chests, guns and all. Neither of them would be moving again real soon.

Then there was the last shooter. He was "hiding" behind a light pole. I webbed his hands to it.

Two cops ran up beside me with guns pointed at the zombie-robbers I had knocked down.

"Nice job, Spider-Man," one cop said.

"Thanks," I said.

The gun-fire had stopped, leaving an odd silence in the street. An unnatural silence for the middle of a city afternoon. Inside the bank I saw that the other zombie robbers had been disarmed and captured.

I did a quick jump up onto the bank wall and scanned the people on the sidewalk and the gawkers who had gathered inside other stores and restaurants watching. None of them looked like our Jewel nutcase.

The two robbers who I had disarmed first had headed down the street in different directions. A block away to my right I could see that the police had gotten one of them. So I went left, figuring to track down the other fugitive.

It took me almost a minute to spot him, walking calmly along the sidewalk as if just out for a normal business afternoon. In his hand was a black bag, filled with bank money.

I was about to swoop down and nab him when my tired brain finally kicked into gear. From the sounds of the note delivered this morning by Hancock, the Jewel had plans of building a crime syndicate. And that would take money. And the zombie robbers seemed to be acting as if they were trying to get away.

If that was the case, maybe this zombie calmly walking below me might just lead me to the Jewel.

I went higher on the side of the buildings and moved along ledges and roof-tops, following him down the street, making sure I wasn't seen by anyone.

Three blocks later he turned right and moved down a side street, then turned into an alley and stopped at a side door to a pawn shop. Without so much as a look around, he turned the knob and went inside.

I dropped like a rock toward that door, and reached it just moments after the zombie closed it behind himself.

I waited a long two count, glancing around to make sure no one was watching me, then eased the door open just enough to duck inside.

My spider-sense didn't buzz, so I knew I was safe—or at least not in any imminent danger.

The place was warm, almost too warm, and smelled of mold and wet cardboard. It was also fairly dark, with only a few bare light bulbs trying to shove the gloom back into the corners. The sound of a television playing somewhere filled the room with pro-wrestling audience cheers.

I moved up one dark wall slowly, silently trying to get to a place where I could see the entire room. As I got above the height of the shelves I was surprised at how big the room was, with high ceilings, and more junk than I had seen in one place in a long time. The aisles were so jammed with stuff that no one could move down them without turning sideways every few feet.

The zombie had moved toward the front of the store and as I watched he sat the black bag on the ground in the middle of twenty or so other suitcases and bags that filled an area of one aisle. Then he headed for the front door.

I had been right. The Jewel now wanted the money from the hold-ups and this was a drop. And a good one, too. That bag fit right in with the others on the floor and shelves.

As the zombie passed the glass case full of guns and cheap jewelry a voice said, "Help you?"

A heavy-set man in cover-alls stood from where he'd been

watching television behind the counter. He wasn't the guy from the pictures, that was for sure.

The zombie seemed to stop, then suddenly look around as if waking up. "Ah—ah, no thanks."

The guy was no longer in zombie state. Clearly he had followed all his directions.

"Where am I?" the guy asked.

The heavyset man behind the counter snorted, then sat back down in front of his wrestling match.

The guy did another quick look around, then darted for the front door as if getting to the street would answer his questions. I doubted it would.

I eased myself into a position on the top of a high shelf that seemed completely in the dark, then tried to make myself comfortable. I had a sneaking hunch I was going to be here for a while waiting for someone to come pick up that bag.

Two hours later I was still waiting, desperately trying to stay awake in the stuffy heat of the store.

During that time I had learned nothing more than the guy who ran the place belched a great deal and didn't seem to know the bag was even there. He had walked past the bag twice on his trips to the bathroom in the back and hadn't noticed it. I was fairly certain he had nothing to do with any of this. The Jewel had simply picked this store as a drop site, more than likely one of many he might try to use around the city.

But if this was a drop site, eventually someone had to come and check to see if anything had been dropped off, then take it to the Jewel. Or maybe even the Jewel himself would show up. And when that happened, I planned on being close by.

Another hour passed and I knew for certain I was going to need help. There was no telling when the bag would be picked up. It might be days. And watching and waiting patiently wasn't one of my strong suits. I was more the wade-into-the-fight-punching type.

At five the guy stood, yawned, and moved to flip the closed

sign on the front door. I yawned with him as he locked the back door, turned off the lights, and then locked the front door behind him, leaving me sitting in the stinking pawn shop in the dark.

Sometimes a person gets to a place in his life when he wonders how he got there. This was one of those times.

I waited ten minutes, then climbed up to a high window that looked out over the alley, jimmied the lock open, and went out into the cold night air. It was the first time in weeks it actually felt good being in the cold snow.

GETTING HELP

Three minutes later I was knocking on Barb's window. She motioned me inside and I sat down in the chair facing her desk, instead of crouching on the back of it.

"You're looking better than this morning," I said. And she was. She'd taken a shower, changed clothes, and combed her hair. Even the rings under her eyes were lighter.

"Thanks, I guess," she said. "How are the police doing on their stakeouts?"

"Haven't heard," I said. "Been on the shelf for the last few hours."

She frowned at me, so I spent the next few minutes telling her about the bank robbery and the pawn shop. At the mention of the pawn shop her eyes brightened and she asked me the exact address.

After I told her she was even more attentive to the last little bit of the story.

"You know this pawn shop?" I asked after I gave her the last details.

She nodded. "A gun matching the type used to kill Bobbie was sold there three days before all this started. Phony name and address on the log and the guy couldn't remember what the person looked like who bought it. Paid cash. I thought it was a dead-end until now."

"Still might be," I said. "Or a nasty coincidence."

"Yeah," she said. "But my instinct tells me it's not. Take a look at this."

She flipped a folder across her desk at me and I opened it up. It was the lab report from the Washington FBI lab where the residue from the melted spot in the alley was sent for testing.

"Can't make head-nor-tails out of most of that," she said.

I wasn't having the same problem.

"Results of eight different lab tests," I said after studying each page for a minute. "All seem to come down to the same conclusions about the stuff."

"You know this type of science?" she asked, surprised.

"I'm not just another pretty face," I said.

She snorted. Then said, "What's the bottom line?"

"Whatever melted that spot is radioactive, basically," I said. "Actually, it seems a combination of different types of radioactivity. Never seen anything like this before."

"Yeah," Barb said, "that's what the police lab man said. He told me the folks in Washington were exceedingly interested in getting their hands on whatever caused that spot."

"I'll bet."

"Dangerous stuff?" Barb asked.

"Highly, from the looks of this report. Who knows what it did to whoever picked it up. Or what it was doing in that alley. More than likely, if Bobbie's killer touched whatever caused that spot, he's already dead."

"I'll make some phone calls to area hospitals checking for radiation poisoning cases."

"Good idea," I said. I closed the file. "But first, I have a request."

"I bet you need my help staking the pawn shop out," she said. "Right?"

"In one," I said. "And I don't think we should bring the police in on this one just yet. If this guy can control people enough to get them to kill, he might be able to control cops, too."

She nodded. "I was wondering what my next step was. Guess you just handed it to me. Meet me on the corner across from the pawn shop in two hours. I'll see what I can put together."

With that she reached for the phone.

I stood and headed for the window. I knew when I had been dismissed and that was a clear dismissal. She was all business. I liked that about her. Hard on the old ego, but still a good trait for a detective.

She dialed her number, then glanced around at me as I opened the window. "Thanks for the concern this morning."

"Thank you for the long night's work," I said.

She shrugged. "It's what I get the big bucks for."

At that moment the person on the other end of her call answered and she turned away from me, again with the last word.

She was really good at that.

GETTING SET UP

I headed back to the *Bugle*. There I quickly learned that things were getting worse instead of better.

A lot worse.

While I was sitting on that shelf in the pawn shop, three undercover police in zombie state had robbed a deli. From what Robbie had discovered, the police had seen the guy in the Sandpines hat and surrounded him on a subway platform. That was the last thing the undercover cops remembered until after they snapped out of the zombie trance.

The police had pulled all their men out of the subways.

"This is getting scary," Robbie said. "What happens if this guy marches into City Hall and wants to take over the city? Who's going to stop him?"

I had no answer for that. What worried me was what happened if this guy could control me as Spider-Man? That was a weapon I didn't want to hand him.

Between the time I checked into the *Bugle* and meeting

Barb, I stopped three more zombie robberies. But as I was doing it I felt as if I was swimming upstream, the river was winning, and I was drowning.

To make things even worse, by the time I swung down to meet Barb on the corner near the pawn shop, the snow had increased and turned wet. The kind of snow that stuck to just about anything like thick cotton candy. If this kept up, I was going to be a very wet super hero by the time the night was out.

Barb was standing under an awning. She saw me as I swung in over the street. I motioned for her to wait, then went carefully in the upper window of the pawn shop. The bag was still there and I eased down on a web line until I was just above it. The first time I was here I hadn't checked to see what was actually in the bag. If Barb and I were going to spend all the time watching it, we should at least know what was in it.

I eased the black bag open just enough so that I could see the money. Wrapped money from the bank.

A half minute later I was on the sidewalk beside Barb.

"Bag full of money is still waiting," I said.

"Good," Barb said pointed to a third story dark window on the corner of the building. "Meet me there." She turned and went quickly inside.

I went up the side of the old brick building and crouched on the thin ledge by the window. From there, even through the thick snow I could see both entrances to the pawn shop, plus down the two streets in both directions.

Inside the room a light clicked on, lighting the old-style drapes. Barb came to the window and unlatched it, letting me in to the sparsely furnished room.

"I'll leave the next window over unlocked so you can come and go," she said as I dropped inside and shook the snow off of me almost like a dog would shake water. "I'll set up my equipment in this window."

"Good spot," I said. "How'd you get it so quick?"

"I have my ways," she said. "I still have to get my photo

equipment and tape recorders up here. Anything that goes on around that pawn shop will be recorded."

"Shifts?"

"From what I've heard has happened with the subway police stakeout, you're going to be needed on the streets more than ever. Am I right?"

"Afraid so," I said.

She nodded. "If you could take this for an hour, I should be able to get the equipment set up in that time."

"No problem," I said. I didn't want to think about what would be happening on the streets during that hour. But at the moment I felt this was our best chance of catching this nutcase.

"Then," Barb said, "If you could spell me for a few hours from say, one in the morning until four, and maybe an hour in the middle of the morning some time, I can handle the rest."

"You sure?"

She nodded. "I've done this before. I know what it takes. Coffee, coffee, and more coffee."

"Okay," I said. "Get your equipment."

She flicked off the light in the room and scooted a chair for me over to the window.

"I'll be back," she said, heading for the door.

"I'll be here," I said.

"Try to be awake," she said as she closed the door behind her.

"Hah! Not a problem," I said to the closed door. But after an hour of sitting in the dark and watching through the falling snow at nothing going on below, staying awake *was* a problem. I was tired. Bone-weary tired. Sitting and watching snow fall and cabs go by didn't thrill me. But I certainly wasn't going to tell her that.

I managed to stay awake until she returned. And for the second time in one day, going out into the cold and snow actually felt good.

Chapter Eleven
Very Little Sleep

For the seven very long days after Barb and I sat up our stake-out on the pawn shop I got almost no sleep. I thought not getting much sleep the first week of the Jewel's reign of terror on the city was bad, the second week made the first seem like full night's. Even with the extra reserves of my spider-strength, I was wearing down like an old battery in a kid's toy.

And that lack of sleep was becoming dangerous. I was missing grabs on sides of buildings, stumbling into desks at the *Bugle,* and almost nodding off every night while I had duty over the pawn shop. I did manage to keep my promise to Mary Jane. Every morning I was home for at least an hour, one day up to three whole hours of sleep. And breakfast. A couple of the days it was the only food I managed to eat.

A long week. Not enough sleep. Here's how it went in a nutshell.

DAY EIGHT

Barb walked through the pawn shop to make sure the bag was still there. It was. Nothing had changed. The owner of the shop only grunted at her.

Around midnight I went in through the window and put a spider-tracer inside the bag just to be sure we could follow it when, or if, it did get moved.

That night the ordinary-citizen zombie robberies slowed. But that was only because the Jewel was using different people. I stopped six robberies where rent-a-cops were the zombies. Two people were injured in those attempts. The Jewel seemed to have no problem finding humans who carried guns. That fact, day after day, kept shocking me. I'm not sure why it shocked me, but it did.

The Jewel also turned two city cops into zombies and had them drive their patrol car into a jewelry shop front window in a botched robbery attempt. No one was hurt.

DAY NINE

No movement of the bag. I checked. The owner of the pawn shop acted like he hadn't even noticed it was there. No surprise in that place. Besides his wrestling matches on television, I doubt the guy knew much of anything.

Around three in the afternoon, as it was snowing hard for the second time that day, I missed a grab at a building's corner just above the sixth floor.

Not enough sleep.

Because of my angle of movement through the air it was too late for me to even fire a web to pull me out. Normally I would have just hit the wall and held on, but this time I smashed through the very center of a large sixth story window into an office full of desks and computers.

I ended up on my back at the feet of a very startled woman in a very short dress. Luckily she couldn't see my red face under my mask as I dove back out the window with a weak, "Sorry."

I couldn't even think of a smart remark for the occasion.

That night I stopped a half dozen zombie robberies and two regular ones. It seemed that the criminals of the city thought the zombies would give them good cover since the police were so busy. By and large they were right. Four robberies, three with zombies, one regular criminals, succeeded without either me or the police getting there in time. Luckily, on the zombie robberies, we got all the money back as the zombies left it in obvious places like park benches or subway trash cans. So far the only bag of loot from a zombie robbery not recovered was the bag in the pawn shop.

The victims of the regular crooks weren't so lucky. They got none of their money back.

DAY TEN

Midtown Manhattan had almost become a war zone. The regular criminals pulled more and more jobs. The zombies got more and more dangerous. More pulled the trigger of their guns. The city jail cells were like rooms in a bad, hour-rate hotel. No zombie stayed long.

The *Bugle,* the TV and radio stations, all warned people to just stay home.

Three people were killed in a shoot-out outside a restaurant just five blocks from the pawn shop.

I was going crazy trying to be in a half dozen places at once.

No one touched the bag of money in the pawn shop.

Mary Jane had to wake me up twice during breakfast.

DAY ELEVEN

Basically more of the same.

Only on day eleven of the Jewel's reign of terror we got another note from him at the Bugle. It said, and I quote:

The fun will continue. Give up trying to stop me. I cannot be stopped.

The note was again on yellow legal paper, this time delivered by a cop who had been guarding Grand Central Station.

Again no one came for the bag in the pawn shop.

DAY TWELVE

No one came for the bag, but a woman zombie robber did enter the pawn shop. And not to rob it.

I was sitting on a ledge, staring down at a crowd of people

emerging from a subway entrance when I felt a slight tingle in my spider-sense. It went off and on and off and on. That was the signal from Barb that she needed me, and fast. I'd modified a spider-tracer so she could contact me with it.

I was only four blocks away from our stake-out and covered the distance while my spider-sense told me she was still calling me. She'd already opened the window and I went in quick, trusting my spider-sense to tell me that I hadn't been seen. She was sitting at a playback monitor for the camera recording the area around the pawn shop.

"Take a look this," she said, pointing at the screen as I entered.

A woman wearing a long coat and high heals even with the snow on the sidewalks, moved up the alley and into the pawn shop back door.

Barb stopped the tape just before the woman disappeared. "Take a look what she has clutched under her arm."

"A black bag," I said. "A little bigger than a purse."

"Exactly," Barb said. She hit the fast forward on the tape until a point where the front door of the pawn shop opened. Then she slowed the tape.

"No bag," I said as the woman came out.

"And watch this," Barb said. "She's confused."

Barb was right. The woman moved a few steps down the sidewalk and then looked around, as if trying to get her bearings. For a moment she stood there, slowly looking around. Then using careful steps as if she were walking on thin ice, the woman moved toward the corner. There she stopped and just stared at the street sign, clearly confused.

"She was a zombie," I said.

"Sure looks that way," Barb said. "Guard the fort. I'm going to look for that bag."

I nodded and sat down in the chair I'd spent what seemed like years in over the last four nights.

Half a minute later Barb came into view crossing the street. She went right in the front door of the pawn shop and I sat, watching. I knew she could take care of herself just fine, but still it felt odd to be sitting and watching while someone else did the dangerous work. Very odd.

Not like me at all.

I glanced at the clock on the monitor at one minute.

Then at two minutes.

At three minutes I was getting worried when the front door of the pawn shop opened. Barb came out, gave me a thumbs-up sign where it wouldn't be seen, and turned in the opposite direction from where she had come. I knew she would go around the corner to the back of the building and come in that way to make sure the pawn shop owner didn't see her. A real pro.

Two minutes and six seconds later she opened the door and came into the room. Nothing but a few cars, one woman walking a dog, and ten cabs had passed on the street below.

"We've got two bags," she said. "The second bag is full of money just like the first."

"Wonder what she robbed to get that bag?"

Barb shrugged. "Could be anything these days."

"So he's going to come for the money," I said.

"Seems that way," she said. "Just depends on when."

It didn't happen that day.

Or that night.

I stopped a dozen more zombie robberies. One woman was wounded by a stray bullet fired from a zombie's gun. I still saw no one wearing the strange golf hat.

DAY THIRTEEN

No one came for the bags.

I got two hours' sleep.

No one was safe from the Jewel's zombie spell and even the police were now afraid to carry guns.

Three petty crooks were captured by the police when the Jewel turned them into zombies and marched them shooting into a neighborhood police station. Luckily no one was hurt, since the crooks ran out of ammunition before they reached the front door.

The robberies were so bad that many stores that had been hit two or three times just closed up until this was solved. It was cheaper for them. I didn't blame them at all. Even the banks went to having no cash on hand and only dealing with checks until this was done.

Still the robberies continued.

Luckily no one was killed on the thirteenth day.

DAY FOURTEEN

The headline in the *Bugle* read: WILL IT EVER END?

Both Barb and I felt the same way. And Mary Jane felt as if she were in jail in our house.

More robberies. No more deaths.

I went into the pawn shop in the middle of the night to make sure both bags were there. They were.

I put a second spider-tracer in the second bag just to be sure. After this long, I wanted to take no chances we'd lose those bags if they were picked up.

The next day, fifteen days after Bobby Miller was killed in an alley, fifteen days after the Jewel started his zombies robbing and killing, it turned out it was lucky I put that extra tracer in that second bag. But sometimes you have to get lucky to be a good detective. At least that's what Barb said.

I wasn't going to disagree with her.

Chapter Twelve
A Mistake

Ten in the morning. Day Fifteen. For a change the snow had stopped, the temperature had come up, and the sun even peeked through the clouds. The streets had almost instantly turned to slush and the paths through the snow piles had become skating rinks for those on the sidewalks. Everything about the day felt different. I hoped that meant something would change on our zombie plague.

I sat inside the "Jewel War Room" as Robbie called it, the big map of the area in front of me. Three days ago we had all just given up on putting pins in the map for locations of robberies. There were just too many. And so many of the same places were getting hit over and over. No pattern had emerged other than the area of hits. But one of the interns had stuck three or four of our best Jewel pictures on the wall beside the map. I swore in one the Jewel was laughing at us.

I'd gotten a few hours of sleep last night. That, another good breakfast with Mary Jane in which I actually managed to stay awake, plus two cups of coffee and I was feeling almost fit. Maybe I was getting used to this schedule. Of course, the snow breaking and the sun coming out had helped a bunch, too.

"Think this is ever going to end?" Robbie asked as he came into the room and sat on the edge of a desk staring at the city map in front of me.

"I do," I said. "Just not a clue when."

"Or how," Robbie said.

"Yeah, that too."

I honestly didn't have any idea how this Jewel nutcase was going to be stopped. He seemed to be able to take over police as easily as regular people. Chances are I wasn't going to be immune to whatever he was doing and that had me big-time worried. The last thing this city needed was a Zombie Spider-Man.

"Sure wish we knew exactly who this guy was," Robbie said. "And if this guy we're taking pictures of is actually the Jewel. Or just someone who likes to watch robberies."

"I'm betting he's our guy," I said, staring at the hooked nose and weird hat of our suspect. "Not a clue why I'm betting that way."

"Call it a hunch, huh?" Robbie said, laughing.

"Yeah, that and a buck will buy me a losing lottery ticket."

"But you're standing by the bet?" Robbie said.

I looked at the photo of the hook-nosed guy beside the map. "Yeah, I am."

Suddenly my spider-sense tingled. Off. On. Off. On.

Barb's signal from the altered spider-tracer I had given her. Something was happening at the pawn shop.

I did my best to get slowly to my feet. I didn't want to let Robbie know I'd gotten any type of signal. "I'm going to go see if I can get some more pictures. With the better light today we might get a better picture of the guy." It was a lame excuse, but the best I could think of right then.

Robbie nodded. "Be careful out there."

"No other way," I said as I went through the door of the war room. As soon as I was out of Robbie's sight, I ran for the stairwell.

Less than a minute later I swung in over the building across from the pawn shop and down into the window, my spider-sense, fortunately, was quiet.

No Barb.

There was a warm cup of coffee sitting beside the stake-out window and the camera equipment. I did a quick inventory of the room. Nothing out of place, no sign of a struggle. Only her coat was gone. And the spider-tracers that had been in the bags were no longer across the street. They were moving.

Someone had picked up the bags.

I went back out the window and to the top of the building, then headed toward Broadway in the direction of the two tracers in the bags, doing my best to pick her distinctive long coat out of the crowds moving along the sidewalks.

Three blocks from the pawn shop I spotted her, moving slowly and carefully along a sidewalk on Broadway. She was being very careful to not be seen, acting as if she was just out for a morning stroll, doing a little window shopping. Clearly she was following whoever had taken the bags.

I stayed along the roof-tops, making sure I wasn't seen also, moving ahead of her a full block until I had a dead fix on the two spider-tracers. It took me a moment to really understand what I was seeing thirty stories below. It was the guy in the Sandpines hat carrying both bags from the pawn shop.

"Looks like I just won the lottery," I said.

Every so often the Jewel glanced around, looking to see if anyone was following him. It was no wonder Barb was almost a block back of him. She was being extra careful.

After what this guy had done over the last two weeks, I was going to be just as careful.

I moved about a block ahead of him and tucked myself into a corner of a roof-top where I could get a clear view of the sidewalk below with little chance he could see me.

He stopped twice, once forcing Barb to cross the street and go into a deli. She was good. There was no way in the world I would have known she was following the guy in the hat. I doubted he suspected her.

Finally the guy crossed the street and with one more look around walked directly into the main entrance of the Crown Vista Hotel.

I dove off the ledge at the exact same moment Barb burst out of the deli door and started to run down the sidewalk.

I broke my free-fall drop with a web on the hotel sign. The webbing deposited me on the hotel roof that extended out over the sidewalk. Quickly I swung over the edge and then dropped down into a group of tourist-looking types moving toward the main door.

Four of them gasped. One young woman said, "Oh, look. Spider-Man."

"Not really," I said. "Just a birthday surprise for my girl-friend. She likes men in costumes."

"Yeah," she said, her voice slightly husky. "So do I."

Then she licked her lips.

Thank heavens by that time the entire group was through the big door and into the lobby. I ducked to the right and behind a large column towering over the main door. The woman gave me a funny look.

"Part of the game," I said in a loud whisper loud enough for her to hear.

She got this faraway look in her eyes, then winked at me and moved on.

I sighed and looked around. The Crown Vista had a huge main lobby extending three stories into the air, flanked by large marble columns. Plants and a large waterfall filled the center area, flanked by a bar on one side and the registration desk on the other. A dozen columns like the one I was hiding behind framed the lobby like poles holding up the upper part of the building.

The guy in the Sandpine's hat hadn't seen me come in. He was threading his way toward the elevators, no longer looking back.

Barb came through the main door to my right. I caught her eye. "Elevators," I said, just loud enough for her to hear.

She nodded without breaking stride.

I flicked a spider-tracer on the hem of her coat. In case something happened to her I wanted to be able to find out where she was.

Before the guy in the Sandpines hat could get on an eleva-tor with the others waiting, Barb had joined the group.

The moment the elevator doors closed on both of them I headed back outside, nodding to the tourists as I went.

I managed to not run from the hotel, but I wanted to.

I got outside, nodded to the doorman, then headed up the side of the hotel, using the spider-tracers in the bags and on Barb's coat to lead me up.

Two stories from the top one tracer stopped. Barb's tracer.

The thirty-second floor.

The other two tracers went on up to the penthouse floor.

I moved cautiously to the window at the end of the hallway and looked in. Barb was standing in the hall by the bank of elevators looking almost angry.

I rapped hard on the window and she frowned, then headed down the hall in my direction.

Of course the window wouldn't open from either side, so she motioned that I meet her down on the side street, then turned and headed back to the elevator.

The other two spider-tracers had stopped on the top floor of the hotel.

And stayed there.

I thought about going up and taking a look in the windows, but there was no point in spooking the guy now that we knew where he was. It had taken us two weeks to get this break. It was better to wait, get some back-up, then I'd take a look.

I dropped back to a ledge three stories above the street and waited there until Barb came out. I could sense from the tracer on her coat that she was in the lobby, but just wasn't coming immediately outside.

Finally, after a long ten minutes, she appeared and looked around, scanning the sides of the buildings for me. When she finally spotted me, she motioned down a side street and headed that way.

A block away from the hotel I dropped down in front of her and we moved behind a staircase to talk. Her face looked pale and she looked shaken, as if she'd just seen some sort of ghost. Or almost got hit by a cab. Both events had the same sort of look.

"He had an elevator key to the upper floor," she said without so much as a hello. "I couldn't follow him all the way up."

"Probably better," I said. "I don't think there's much up there except a penthouse. You would have been pretty obvious."

She nodded. "He was creepy. I rode the last two floors with just him and me."

At that she shuddered.

Seeing a woman as strong as Barb shudder wasn't something that boosted my confidence.

"I could go up and take a look in the windows," I said. "From the tracers in the bags, I can tell they're still up there."

Barb shook her head. "I think we need to let the police try to take it from here. I stopped at the front desk and got the strangest response."

She took a deep breath before going on. "The front desk says the penthouse rooms have been booked for almost two weeks."

"Two weeks?" I asked. "That's an interesting coincidence." It had been exactly two weeks since Bobby was killed. And the first zombie robbery.

She nodded. "So I asked who had booked the rooms. The manager behind the desk actually looked confused at the question. His eyes sort of went blank and he repeated that the penthouse was booked."

"The guy's turned the hotel staff into zombies," I said.

"Seems that way," she said.

"This guy is flat dangerous," I said. "We've got to figure out how he's getting control over people."

"We're not going to find that out until we capture him."

"Can we capture him without knowing?"

"Catch-22," she said. "But let's give the police the first shot at him. We'll play back-up."

"Agreed," I said. Better not to tell her what I was really thinking—that now that I knew where he was, I was going to get the Jewel.

She pulled a cell-phone from her jacket pocket and quickly tapped in a number. Then while she was waiting she said, "I'll watch the front of the building until they get here. Can you watch as much of the side and back as you can? And, promise me you won't try anything."

What should I tell her, that I *was* planning something? That I *was* going to go in and take down the Jewel before he could control and hurt any more innocent people? I could have given her some flip comment about not trying something crazy—which had a different meaning coming from Spider-Man.

But, the way she looked at me, the way you could see how she thought about Bobby and how she didn't want me to end up the same way, it reminded me of how my late aunt May would look at me when she thought I was getting sick. That look Barb gave me lasted only a second, if that long. The tough dame had the soul of a tender woman hidden deep inside. Something must have hurt her a long time ago.

Something—or someone. The death of her husband, or worse?

I knew that, right now anyway, I couldn't add to that hurt. I'd go up and just watch. Just this once.

The police would get their chance. If it didn't work, then I'd make my move.

Chapter Thirteen
First Assault

The police came in slow and quiet. After fifteen minutes I could see the entire building was surrounded by double layers of police and they were slowly, but calmly, getting people out of the lobby area of the hotel. I was impressed.

I swung down onto the sidewalk when I saw Sergeants Hawkins and Drew talking with Barb. Both of them nodded to me.

"I've explained to them what happened with the bags," Barb said. "And who we followed with them."

"The bags are still up there," I said. "I know that much. Can't guarantee the money or the man, though."

"Good work, you two," Hawkins said.

I have a sneaking hunch that even through my mask it was clear I was flat shocked. I could count on one hand the number of times the police had actually complimented me. It was not something I ever expected.

"Now we got to see if we can stop this character," Barb said. "That's going to be the hard part."

"Agreed," Hawkins said.

"I say we take about twenty men and just go up there and arrest him," Drew said.

"I doubt he's going to just let you," I said. "Not after what he's been doing to the police and general public the last two weeks. Remember."

Barb nodded her agreement.

"Yeah," Drew said, "but are we going to know that until we try? Maybe we can get him by surprise, so whatever he does to make people into zombies isn't working."

"Good point," Hawkins said. "There are four entrances up there. Go in from four directions and he can't control them all."

"You hope," I said.

Hawkins glanced at Barb.

She only shrugged.

"We do it," Hawkins said. "We'll keep up the double para-meter around the building. Drew, you take ten men and go up there and see what happens."

Without another word, Drew turned and headed toward the hotel, indicating police officers that should come with him.

The police went up both elevators and both stairwells. I watched from the top of a nearby building, trying to catch a glimpse of what was happening in there. Again it felt real odd to not be in the center of the fight. But again, this time it was better to hold back and just watch.

And learn.

And learn I did. What I saw through those windows scared me.

Ten cops went in armed, ready to fire.

They went in quickly, and all at once.

They went in from four different directions. Perfectly timed and executed.

It should have worked.

It didn't.

Suddenly they all just stopped as if their feet had become glued to the carpet.

Slowly they all stood up straight, as if at attention, then put their guns away, and filed out to the elevators like a well-behaved class of children.

I shuddered.

Through one window I could see the Jewel guy laughing. It was the same guy with the weird Sandpines golf hat. The same guy we had tailed with the bags from the pawn shop. It looks like, for the first time, we had a positive identification of the Jewel.

Right at that moment there was no doubt in my mind that we were up against one of the most dangerous people I'd ever come across. Right now I'd much rather face the Green Gob-lin, or even Carnage. At least I knew how to fight them. I had no idea with this guy.

He hadn't touched those men. He hadn't even been that close to them. Yet he controlled them like puppets. And I had no doubt at all he could do it to me, too, if I let him.

As the ten cops got on the elevator, I dove for the main entrance of the hotel.

Barb and Sergeant Hawkins were just inside the front door.

"Drew and his men are coming down the elevator," I said as I burst into the hotel lobby. "All ten of them. I watched the guy we trailed simply take over their minds without touching them."

"Take over their minds?" Hawkins asked.

"That's what it looked like to me," I said.

"All ten of them?" Barb said.

"All ten," I said. "All at once."

Barb stared at me as if I were nuts. I wished I was right at that moment.

"Blast it," Hawkins said, pulling his gun and indicating the police near the elevators should take cover.

I went up a column to get a better angle at the opening of the elevators as Barb drew her gun and followed Hawkins, moving into a position behind a large planter that gave her a good angle at the elevators. I figure I could disarm three or four of the cops with webs before they had time to even get off a shot.

That elevator seemed to take forever to get to the ground floor. What were we thinking sending ten armed men into the Jewel's hands? For two weeks he'd been using armed people to kill and rob others. So we give him more armed people? Totally nuts.

The elevator door seemed to open in slow motion.

I wasn't sure what I was expecting, but when Sergeant Drew just walked out and turned for the front door as if nothing was wrong, I realized I'd been holding my breath.

Hawkins stepped out from behind a planter, gun pointed at his partner. "Just hold it there, Drew."

The other police swarmed out of hiding and took the ten

cop's guns out of their holsters almost before any of them could move.

I dropped down beside Hawkins and Barb.

"What's going on?" Drew asked.

"You tell us," Barb said. "What happened up there?"

Drew got this funny look on his face, then said the most chilling words I had heard in a long time. "Up where?"

Barb glanced at me, then Hawkins. Hawkins was standing, staring at his partner, his mouth actually open.

Finally Hawkins pulled himself together. "You and these men went up to see if you could arrest the guy in the penthouse. You just got off the elevator. What happened?"

Now Drew's face really looked pained as he fought against something inside his head. Finally he said softly, "I don't know."

Hawkins nodded. "I think we better put you and your men in safe keeping for a short time, to make sure the guy up there didn't plant any suggestions."

I couldn't have agreed more. There was a real good chance these cops, in an hour or so, might suddenly become zombies. Better to have them in a safe cell if that happened then walking the streets with guns.

Drew nodded slowly. "Good idea. Take it easy here."

He motioned for the men who went up to the penthouse to follow him as other officers escorted them across the lobby.

Behind Hawkins the elevator dinged and the doors opened. Without thinking, I jumped to a position on the wall above the elevator door.

Both Hawkins and Barb drew their guns.

An elderly couple got out of the elevator, looking confused at all the police, drawn guns, and the almost empty lobby.

"Sorry," Hawkins said, holstering his gun and motioning for an officer to help the elderly couple out. I dropped down beside Hawkins. The woman gave me a very dirty look as she walked past.

I followed Hawkins and Barb back into the center of the lobby.

"You're sure the picture we have of the guy in the hat is this same guy?" Hawkins asked me.

"Absolutely certain," I said. "He turned your partner into a zombie while I watched from across the street."

"And he didn't see you?" Barb asked.

"I'm not sure what would have happened if he had," I said. And I wasn't. I had no idea how this guy did what he did. Or what kind of range he had. Or anything for that matter.

"How are we going to get to this psycho?" Hawkins asked, stopping and looking around. At least forty police were in positions around the lobby and I knew there were at least twice that many outside around the hotel.

At that moment a rather large man in an expensive-looking suit walked up to us. He clearly worked for the hotel in some position of power or another. Barb glared at him, but he ignored her as if she were just a planter.

"Sergeant Hawkins," the man said. "May we let our customers and staff back into this area now?"

"I don't think that—"

The man didn't let Hawkins finish. "Any more delay won't be tolerated. I've been cooperative, but I have a very large hotel to run here. So unless you have a court order, please tell your men to let my customers back inside."

"I can get one," Hawkins said, facing the man squarely.

"Then do it," the manager said. "But until then, I expect to do business as usual."

"Let's just hope no one gets killed in here," Hawkins said.

"That's your job to make sure it doesn't happen," the manager said. "It's my job to run this hotel. I've helped you as much as I can."

At that the man turned and headed for the front door.

"Great," Hawkins said. "How much do you want to bet those were the Jewel's instructions?"

"We just take the Jewel on the street," Barb said. "More than likely a lot safer."

"If we can get him out on the street," Hawkins said, turning and following the manager toward the front door.

GOOD IDEA

After hanging around the hotel area for the next hour, I was satisfied the police, with Barb's help, had the situation under the best control they could. Or anyone could for that matter. If the Jewel guy came outside and didn't surrender when asked, he would be shot by long range snipers stationed in windows and rooftops. The guy wasn't going to be riding the subways again anytime soon.

I headed back for the *Bugle,* ending up in the Jewel war room with Robbie and a reporter named Carl Hanks, telling them what I'd seen down at the hotel. Of course, most of it I said Spider-Man had told me he'd seen.

"How are they going to get the Jewel out of there?" Robbie asked. "The police don't have the manpower to stake out that hotel for a week, let alone a month or more."

"Can't they just gas him out?" Carl asked. Carl was in his forties, had thinning blond hair, and seemed to always look at the negative side of every story. He was also one of the best writers on the Bugle staff. His stories might seem negative, but they were never dull.

"More than likely," I said, "he'd just stay inside the hotel, taking over other guests and employees to help him."

"And the hotel is, of course, doing business as usual," Robbie said.

"So what then? Carl said. "They could first evacuate the entire building, then gas him out."

"Trust me," I said. "From what Spider-Man said he saw, the guy took over ten armed cops coming at him from four directions in a large area of the penthouse. They'd have to gas the entire hotel to force him outside into a big enough area to deal with him. And that's a big hotel."

"Yeah," Carl said, nodding to himself. "Wouldn't work."

"I'm still coming back to the puzzle of how to get the Jewel out into the open, where he can be taken," Robbie said.

Suddenly I knew exactly how to do it. Sort of one of those lightbulb moments.

"How about telling the world where he is," I said.

Robbie sort of looked at me with a puzzled expression.

Carl just said, "Huh?"

"What would happen," I said, "if tomorrow morning the Jewel was delivered a paper that had his picture on the front page, his location detailed out, how the police have the building surrounded, even about the money he got that had been hidden in the pawn shop? And the headline is something like JEWEL CORNERED LIKE A RAT."

Robbie whistled.

"You'll just make him mad," Carl said. "From the sounds of this guy's ego in those notes, he thinks he's in charge."

"Exactly," I said, smiling at Robbie.

Slowly, Robbie started to smile back.

"Carl, start writing," Robbie said. "Peter, you get those interns pulling the best pictures. Then you head back to the Plaza and get some more pictures of the building."

"And tell the police in charge what we're up to?" I asked.

"Of course," Robbie said. "But unless they have a massive objection, we're running with it."

Thirty minutes later, as Spider-Man, I swung down beside Barb and Sergeant Hawkins and told them the *Bugle*'s plan.

Barb only smiled.

Hawkins actually laughed.

Then he said, "We'll even give a copy of the morning paper to that jerk hotel manager a half hour before the Jewel gets his copy, to give Mr. Manager a chance to get ready."

"Oh, you're so nice today, Hawkins," Barb said.

"You're right," Hawkins said, trying not to smile. "Fifteen minutes."

I laughed at the joke.

The next morning it wasn't so funny.

Chapter Fourteen
A Very Public Madman

The night was like a vacation. A normal night. No zombies at all. Seems the money had made the Jewel happy enough to take a night off. Lucky for us, sort of. The police didn't have a chance to get him when he tried to leave the hotel. But no one else was hurt, either.

A night without zombies was heaven. I'd almost forgotten what it was like, it had been so long.

I stopped three robberies, all petty idiots who thought the zombie robberies would continue and give them cover. By midnight I had checked in with the police at the hotel, then from across the street did a quick scouting mission of the penthouse. All the lights were out. Looked like the Jewel had gone to bed.

Barb hadn't. She was still there, beside Hawkins, as if in charge of the police operation.

I talked to the two of them for a short time, then I went home to a very surprised and happy Mary Jane. By one in the morning I was in bed. The alarm rousted me out a half hour before daylight.

Five hours of sleep. Still not a full night's worth, but I wanted to take no chances on missing the Jewel's reaction after seeing the morning paper. It had his picture front page center, with his exact location in the hotel and how he had taken the two bags of money from the pawn shop. The article with the picture also called him petty and insane. He was not going to be happy.

And that was the point.

By sunrise I was stationed on a ledge of a building across from the Crown Plaza Hotel. The morning was bitterly cold and gray overcast. Everything seemed frozen. After crawling out of that nice warm bed next to Mary Jane, I might as well have been swinging between icebergs.

Barb was again beside Sergeant Hawkins when I had arrived. But she had gone home at some point, since she was wearing different clothes. Boots, and a much heavier coat. Even though no link had been established between the Jewel and Bobbie's killing, she had taken on this case with a passion. Clearly she thought there was a link and she was going to chase it until she proved otherwise. And if it turned out the Jewel guy was responsible for Bobbie's death, she was going to chase him to the end of the earth. Of that, I had no doubt.

She and Hawkins had seen the contents of the morning newspaper. Barb told me they both loved it.

Hawkins had increased the police presence around the building to almost double. He had snipers in almost a dozen places, all ready to stop the Jewel if given the order. As far as I could see, Sergeant Drew had not returned to duty yet. They were being very safe.

Barb and Hawkins remained just off the street inside a doorway across from the front door of the hotel.

I moved up to a ledge on the same building.

Two hours we waited.

Two, long, cold hours I stayed on that ledge, my hands tucked under my arms, my feet slowly turning to blocks of ice.

On the street below the traffic increased, as well as the number of people going and coming from the Crown Plaza front and side doors. By seven-thirty it was a normal morning rush hour, right down to the honking taxis and crowded sidewalks.

But no Jewel appeared.

Finally at eight I gave up and headed for the *Bugle*. There was warmth and coffee there. And right at that moment I needed both desperately.

Five minutes later, with my hands wrapped around a hot cup, I wandered through the newsroom toward the "Jewel War Room." The newsroom was fairly quiet compared to the streets and sidewalks outside. The next deadline was hours away.

In the small war room all the pins had been cleared from the city map as if all those zombie crimes had suddenly never happened. Only Robbie was in there, feet up, staring at the now empty map like a television.

"So far it's not working, boss," I said as I scooted a chair around and sat down facing him. "The Jewel's not coming out."

"I know," Robbie said. "He was delivered a paper around six this morning and the hotel security checked back in the hall around six-thirty and he, or someone, had picked it up."

I nodded. Sergeant Hawkins had told Spider-Man the same thing earlier.

"Not sure what I expected, actually," Robbie said.

"I was hoping he'd get mad and storm out of the building," I said. "With as many police as they have stationed around that hotel, he wouldn't have gotten far."

"True," Robbie said.

"We just wait, now," I said, sipping the hot coffee. The chill from the morning's stake-out was finally starting to wear off. I could actually feel my toes again.

At the door of the war room the intern named Rich appeared. He was looking breathless and a little white in the face. "Boss. There's trouble downstairs. I think you better come take a look at this."

Robbie nodded and stood with a sigh. "What kind of trouble."

"Mob trouble," Rich said.

"Mob?" I said, jumping up to follow them.

"In front of the building," Rich said. "Weird bunch."

When we got to the big ground floor lobby of the *Bugle* building I could see what Rich had been talking about. About forty or so people had formed a group that extended along the sidewalk in front of the *Bugle* and a little into the street. They stood shoulder to shoulder, just staring at the *Bugle*'s front door, not moving. Regular pedestrians were moving past the crowd between them and the *Bugle*'s large glass front.

Inside the *Bugle* a group was gathering at the windows. Seeing the crowd outside my spider-sense warned me they were dangerous. Very dangerous. Then finally I caught onto why.

"Zombies," I said to Robbie. "They're all zombies."

"Oh, no," Robbie said. He moved quickly back to the open staircase that went up to the mezzanine of the big room. About ten steps up he stopped and turned, taking charge of the growing crowd inside the front doors of the *Bugle*. "Everyone listen to me." His voice carried over the entire lobby area.

Eyes turned to stare at where we stood on the front staircase. The area almost quieted to complete silence with only the street noise barely noticeable.

"That is a crowd of zombies," Robbie said, his voice strong as he pointed out through the front door. "I want everyone away from those windows and doors and upstairs. Quickly, but orderly. Security, be ready for an attack. Get everyone away from all the floors down here quickly. If you need to leave the building, do it through the back."

Instantly the silent lobby was awash with noise, talking, and movement. Almost everyone who worked for the *Bugle* was in some fashion used to hectic situations, deadlines, or tense situations. No one panicked, but everyone moved.

"I'll get on the phone to the police," I said to Robbie. "Get us some help here."

"Great," he said, standing his ground on the staircase.

I turned and ran up the stairs. I'd do better then just call the police. I'd go report what was happening to Hawkins, then get back here as Spider-Man and help if anything happened.

When I swung off the roof of the *Bugle*, the zombie mob below had grown to almost a hundred.

I found Barb and Sergeant Hawkins thirty seconds later a few blocks away on the sidewalk in front of the hotel. "We got problems," I said as I swung down beside them.

"What kind of problems?" Hawkins asked, looking about as annoyed as a cop could look.

Even Barb frowned.

I knew that watching a large hotel was enough of a problem. They didn't need some wall-crawler to come dropping in with more. But I didn't really have a choice.

"There's a mob of zombies forming in front of the *Bugle*, maybe at least a hundred strong so far."

"What?" Hawkins said.

"Damn," Barb said. "We wanted a reaction and we got it. Just not the right one."

"The *Bugle*'s going to need police to guard it," I said. "And see if we can snap this mob out of their zombie state. I'm heading back there now."

"So how'd he get out of there?" Hawkins said, angry, looking at the hotel.

I pointed at all the people flowing in and out through the front door of the hotel. "He didn't need to leave the building. He's got thousands of people in there to do his work out here for him."

"I was afraid of that," Barb said.

Hawkins nodded. "I'll call in the problem at the *Bugle* and get help on the way. Then we'll get a judge to shut down this hotel."

"The faster you do it," I said, "the less chance of someone getting hurt or killed."

"To hell with the judge," Hawkins said. "I'll close the place first and then get permission." He and Barb started across the street.

At that I headed at full speed back to the *Bugle*. I was really glad I wasn't that hotel manager right about now. With Barb and Hawkins that mad, he wasn't going to know what hit him.

BATTLE OF THE *BUGLE*

I was almost too late.

The zombie crowd had grown even larger, now blocking the sidewalk and most of the street. Cabs were honking as if their horns could move the people. There were already two cops on the scene trying to break up the crowd, having just about as much luck as the cab horns.

As I swung down over the growing crowd my spider-sense went nuts.

Everyone in front of the *Bugle* was silent, standing like soldiers at attention, side by side, staring with blank eyes at the building's front door.

It was like a bad movie, only much creepier.

And much more dangerous.

Through the front windows I could see Robbie still on the stairs preparing the defense. A half-dozen security cops were stationed at different places in the lobby. Otherwise everyone else was out of sight.

I swung down to the two beat cops who were trying to get two guys to move away without luck.

"They're zombies," I said. "The entire mob is made up of zombies."

"No way," one cop said, then actually looked at the eyes of the guy he'd been trying to move. He stepped back as if hit with an electrical shock.

"They're going to need help inside if the mob attacks," I said. "I've already got more police help on the way."

"Good work, Spider-Man," one cop said as both he and his partner headed at a run to get inside the *Bugle*.

I shook my head in amazement. Twice in one week I had been complimented by the police. What was I doing wrong?

I jumped up on the side of the building overlooking the front door. From there I could see everyone in the crowd. So far there were no guns in sight. But I had a sneaking hunch there might be a few in this bunch. I figured my job was going to be to disarm the zombies as fast as I could see the guns. I just hoped Robbie had informed his guards to shoot low, for the legs and feet, if they had to fire. No point in killing innocent people when wounding them would stop them just as quickly.

Then I realized what I had been thinking. There was no point in shooting any zombie. They were just innocent people. There had to be another way out of this.

The zombie crowd grew as more came from the direction

of the Crown Plaza and suddenly stopped and faced the *Bugle* building. A few regular people seemed to try to shove through the zombie mob, not having much success.

I motioned a few of them to turn around and get out of there. They did.

The minutes seemed to tick past slowly.

The faces staring at me were as cold and blank as a gray winter day.

My spider-sense was buzzing like an angry bee, warning me to get away. I would have gladly been a hundred other places than in front of a mob of blank-faced people. I was going to have nightmares about this for years.

Cab drivers shouted and blew their horns.

The zombies stayed rooted in place, faces blank.

I stuck to the cold side of the building, watching.

Finally, just as two police cars managed to get to the intersection a block away, the zombies moved almost in mass. Like a poorly trained marching band, they all took a step forward.

Now my spider-sense really went wild.

I dropped down onto the sidewalk in front of the zombies.

They took another halting step toward the building.

Then I turned back to face the massive crowd moving to smash me between the building and their own bodies.

I could see six guns drawn from coats and purses.

I managed to get two of them with pin-point web shots before the first bullet smashed the window of the *Bugle* building behind me. I webbed two more guns out of zombie hands.

Another shot smashed into a window.

I got that gun, then shoved two men in the first line of people. They stumbled backwards into the people behind them. Instantly I saw the life come back into their eyes.

"You were zombies," I shouted at both as I took a woman gently by the shoulders and shook her. She instantly came out of the zombie state.

"Start waking up the people around you," I said. "Quickly."

One man nodded and did as I said. The other man and the woman just looked puzzled.

Another shot was fired at the building.

With a quick bounce off the roof of the entrance to the *Bugle* building, I was in front of the man with the gun. An instant later I had the gun out of his hands.

"Didn't you read the paper? Don't carry a gun into a city."

The guy looked confused, but there was life in his eyes again.

I shook the guy beside him. Then the next. Then the next person.

It was working. Those that I shook were out of the zombie state.

A little old woman was in line, staring blankly at the front door of the *Bugle*. I shook her lightly. "Time to wake up," I said. Then I snatched her out of line and placed her against the wall out of danger of getting trampled by those behind her.

My shake woke her up.

Robbie had seen what I was doing.

Behind me, Robbie, the guards and cops, guns holstered and strapped into place, were pouring out of the front door of the *Bugle* and wading into the crowd, yelling, shaking, doing anything they could to wake up the crowd.

Strangest battle I had ever seen. One side pushing forward trying to get inside a building, the other side shaking them to wake them up.

Weird. Just plain weird.

And silent. Only the honking cabs and the distant sound of the city filled the cold air. Otherwise this mob fight was deadly silent.

One by one we shook people, waited until life came back to the zombie's eyes before moving them out of the way and going after the next in line.

Some of the once-zombies even caught on to the defense and joined in.

I jumped up to the cover of the entrance way so I could see out over the crowd. Right away I saw three zombies who were carrying guns, but hadn't reached a position yet to get a clear shot at the *Bugle* building.

I got all three of those guns yanked out of their hands.

Then I dropped down into an area of zombies that was threatening to shove Robbie and his men back into the building and helped with the shaking defense.

Rich, Kelly, and Jeff came out of the front door, all holding cameras. They spread out, staying along the building and snapping pictures as if there were no tomorrow. Robbie was going to be mad when he saw them, but it was good they were doing what they were doing. I hadn't had the time to even set up my camera.

Another shot smashed into the window of the *Bugle*.

All the cops and guards instantly went for their guns.

"Keep them holstered," I shouted as I did a handspring over a few zombies and yanked the gun out of a woman's hand. Then I shook her hard enough to bring light back to her eyes.

"The police will want to talk to you about that shot you just fired."

She looked around, then turned as white as the snow beside the building.

I handed her gun to her and pointed at the police car. "Please wait there."

She nodded.

One cop beside me growled at her. "Make sure you do as the web-slinger said."

Again she just nodded. I doubted she'd ever carry a gun again.

I jumped back up to the entrance cover and scanned the crowd. This time I saw and disarmed two more dangerous zombies of their weapons.

The fight was nothing short of surreal.

A movie without a soundtrack.

The zombies were silent.

Robbie and his troops of shakers were only grunting from the exercise of shaking.

Two women were crying, sitting against the front wall of the *Bugle,* clearly in shock at waking up on the street. I had to admit, that would mess up a person.

The zombies attacking the *Bugle* building still covered the sidewalk and the entire street. Over the first minute of the silent, shaking "fight," we had managed to wake up maybe a hundred of them. But there were hundreds and hundreds more to go.

I did a quick scan for guns of the rows of zombies closest to the lead edge. Nothing. So I dropped down beside Robbie and did my share of shaking the zombie. It sounded like a bad carnival game: Shake the Zombie: Win a Prize.

Only this was no game.

And was no fun.

One at a time I shook another human, making sure he or she was awake, then moving them aside to do the same to the next zombie in line.

No zombie tried to defend themselves.

No zombie threw a punch.

It seemed to go on forever.

By the time the afternoon was over I had taken forty-two guns out of the mob. And shaken seemingly hundreds and hundreds of zombies. The supply of zombies dried up right around four, as Hawkins and Drew finally got the Crown Plaza Hotel bottled up.

By the best estimates, over seven hundred zombies attacked, for lack of a better way of putting it, the *Bugle* building. The headline the next morning had photos of the battle from the three interns and the headline read: BUGLE . . . 1: JEWEL . . . 0.

Sounded good, but the most important battles were yet to come. And I'd say even though we had him outnumbered, and now knew where he was, the advantage was to the Jewel.

Chapter Fifteen
A Long Fall

The area around the Crown Plaza hotel now looked more like a war zone than a city street. The police had everything closed off for at least one block in all directions. Barricades blocked the streets, police in riot gear patrolled the perimeter. All businesses inside the area were closed, all parked cars had been moved or towed. No car, no person was getting through.

Swinging in from the battle of the *Daily Bugle* building, I counted at least ten cops in windows with high powered rifles. There was no doubt now that the police were not going to give this Jewel guy a chance to escape.

If they could help it. With this guy, there was no telling what a person could do. Or not do.

After shaking a few hundred normal people out of their zombie state, the thought of the Jewel getting a grip on my mind scared me to death. There was no telling what he'd do with me before he was finished. And my reputation with the city was just slowly starting to get better. Plus with my mask they wouldn't be able to tell by my eyes that I was in a zombie state.

So my choice was simply not let him get into my mind and do whatever he did to make people zombies.

It was my only choice. The alternative wasn't thinkable.

Barb stood sipping a cup of coffee just outside the front door of the hotel. She was alone on the empty sidewalk, her coat slightly open and flapping in the slight wind.

"You lost your sidekick Hawkins," I said as I dropped down beside her.

She tipped her head at the front door. "Inside with Drew."

"So zombie boy is back, huh?" I said.

"Don't let him hear you call him that," Barb said, laughing. "He's a little touchy about not being able to remember what happened up there."

"Don't blame him."

She sipped on her coffee, then said, "Real battle at the *Bugle,* I hear."

"Not fun," I said. "We managed to get out of it with a few broken windows and a lot of really, really confused people."

"Lucky no one got killed."

"Very lucky," I said.

It actually felt that for the first time we had the Jewel in a draw position. He couldn't come down and get more zombies. We couldn't go up and get him.

Draw. Stalemate.

Six cops emerged from the building with Hawkins and Drew right behind them.

"Building is as empty as a church on New Year's Eve," Hawkins said.

"Only the guy in the penthouse," Drew said.

"You sure he's still up there? Barb asked.

Hawkins shrugged. "Not sure about anything with this guy. Are we, Drew?"

Drew's face turned slightly red, but he said nothing.

"How about I give the penthouse a little once-over?" I said. "See what I can see up there."

"From the outside?" Barb asked, looking worried.

"From the outside," I said.

Hawkins glanced at Barb, then nodded. "I'll alert my men in the surrounding buildings what you're going to do."

Finally Hawkins gave me the thumbs-up from across the street.

"Back shortly," I said to Barb and jumped to the side of the hotel.

"Be careful," she said.

"I'll be home for dinner," I said.

"I can't cook," she said.

Again she got the last word because by then I was too far up the side of the hotel.

It didn't take me long to climb to the top. The penthouse area was actually only about one quarter of the size of the entire building, sitting up there like a building on top of a building. This hotel was the highest building around. And the Jewel had the top of that. Sort of like *King of the Hill.*

On the west side of the hotel roof there was a small garden and large patio with bare trees in large planters. The east and north sides of the penthouse simply looked out over the city, set back slightly from the main edge of the building just enough on both sides to allow a small balcony area. Since it was winter, all the patio furniture and chairs were missing from all the rooftop.

My guess was the entire penthouse area, including the elevators and service sections, was about the size of a normal house in the suburbs. I had no idea what such a large suite in the center of the city rented for, but I was sure the Jewel wasn't paying the going rate. Or any rate at all, for that matter.

I went all the way to the top between two windows and first studied the roof of the penthouse. It was just like most other city building roofs. Some standard equipment and a door leading down into what most likely was a maintenance area in the elevator core. Nothing special and nothing had been recently added.

The door was solidly locked. And there was no where for the Jewel to go if he came up here.

I moved to the west side and eased myself down over the edge of the building, crawling down the wall so that just the top of my head and eyes extended down over the top of the window.

A bedroom. The huge bed was unmade, the television was out of its cabinet, but not turned on. A dozen or so hotel towels were tossed in a pile in the corner.

"Doesn't like maid service," I said softly, then backed up the wall away from the window.

The next window looked into a large dining-room-type area, with a large oak table, a dozen chairs, and a large chandelier filling the center of the room. Pizza boxes littered the table and at least two dozen paper Coke cups.

No sign of the Jewel.

"What a slob," I said, again backing up the wall away from the window.

The next window over, my spider-sense kicked in really hard, even before I poked my head far enough below the top of the window to see. I could tell from the spider-tracers that the two bags were in this room, as well as something else very, very dangerous.

I wanted to pull back and just get off this roof. But I had no choice. I'd come up here to scout out the Jewel and that was what I was going to do.

I eased myself a little lower until I could just barely see the room. It was like a large office, with a desk and three or four chairs. The two bags from the pawn shop had been tossed against one wall and the money from the bags was stacked in neat piles on the corner of the desk. It looked like quite a bit. It hadn't seemed that much when in the bags.

The Sandpines golf hat was sitting on top of the piles of money as if it was shading the president's faces on those bills from the room's bright light.

A man sat at the desk, his back to the window. He was wearing the same clothes as the guy we had trailed. He had dark hair, slicked back and clearly dirty.

The Jewel.

I couldn't tell what he was working on, but my spider-sense was going wild. This guy was as dangerous as a bullet heading my way. Maybe even more so.

With his back turned toward me.

Fighting the desire to duck away that my spider-sense was sending through me, I watched him for what seemed like an eternity, but in reality was only a few seconds.

Then, as if sensing I was there, he turned around.

And looked up directly at me.

His eyes were green.

Bright green.

Radioactive green.

Glowing green eyes that seemed to suck me into them, growing larger and larger.

My spider-sense went completely wild.

Instantly I let go of the building.

I had to get away from him.

From those eyes.

I had to.

I dropped past the penthouse window like a rock.

But I was too late.

The inside of my head had become a battle ground.

It was as if a thousand, slimy green snakes had crawled inside my head and were slithering around inside my mind. And every snake had large, glowing green eyes.

I fought, retreating inside myself, kicking at the snakes, throwing them back, not letting them in.

The snakes searched for control, searched for how to take my mind.

I fell.

Past the next floor, brushing a balcony ledge, falling.

I could feel my spider-sense screaming its warning.

The green snakes slowly won, taking more and more of my mind under their control.

The eyes seemed to cover me, the green slime seemed to give me nothing to hold onto.

"No!" I shouted at the snakes, kicking at them, grabbing their slimy bodies, throwing them away.

Yet there were too many.

I could feel it.

I could sense it.

I was losing.

Falling.

Frozen by the battle in my head.

But there had to be a way.

I couldn't become a zombie.

The snakes, green, glowing, slimy, their eyes wide and glowing, attacked my every thought.

There was no pain.

I kicked.

I screamed at them.

I continued to fall.

They were winning.

Slowly, surely taking over my mind, planted there by one glance from the Jewel.

The upper floors of the hotel were starting to flash past.

I would hit the street and bounce, very dead.

Then the snakes would be gone from my mind.

I would win with my death.

The snakes seemed to hesitate, as if the thought stopped them, then they renewed their attack on my mind; faster and faster, as if the they didn't like the idea of my dying anymore than I did.

Pain.

That was the answer.

Pain cleared the control out of other zombies. If shaking did it, pain would do it.

Suddenly in the battle for control of my mind I seemed to be holding them off.

I had to move.

I eased one finger toward my web-shooters.

The snakes fought me.

I remembered pain.

I focused the memories of that pain at the snakes.

I remembered what it felt like to be hit by Carnage.

I remembered the pain of the death of Uncle Ben.

That pain was the biggest of all, because I blamed myself for his death.

The snakes seemed to retreat.

I regained some control. I hoped, deep inside the fortress of my mind, that it was enough.

My finger closed on the trigger for my web-shooter as it had done thousands of times before.

Only this time it seemed to happen in slow motion. And was a great victory.

The next events seemed to happen in an instant.

My web-shooter fired.

The web caught a railing, then like a pendulum, I slammed

into the side of the hotel with more force than I had hit anything in a long, long time.

The wind was knocked out of me.

But, the snakes were gone.

And the eyes.

Vanished instantly from my mind as if never there.

I fired another web at the building across the street.

That second web let me swing down to the concrete, where I hit and rolled, ending up with my back against a streetlight.

I was hurting in more places than I could remember hurting. My costume was ripped on the shoulder and my arm was bleeding into my glove

But I was alive.

And in control of my own mind. And after the last few seconds, that felt wonderful.

Chapter Sixteen
Wow! What a Headache

Barb, Hawkins and Drew all came running to me. I had managed to push myself into a sitting position in the snow, my back against the light pole. My head hurt as if my entire brain had been removed, twisted and squeezed, and then shoved back inside my skull through my ear. Twice.

"You all right?" Barb asked, kneeling down in front of me as Hawkins and Drew stood back in the center of the street, guns drawn. I didn't blame them. They couldn't take any chances that I was a zombie.

"I've been worse," I said. "I just can't remember exactly when or where."

"Is he a zombie?" Drew asked.

"Takes one to know one," I said.

"I think he's fine," Barb said, smiling at me.

"Not so sure about fine," I said. "Alive covers it better. Help me up."

Barb extended a gloved hand and pulled me fairly gently to my feet. I stood there, feeling happy with the solidness of the street under me. I did a quick check to see if any of those green snakes with the big eyes were still hanging around inside my head. Didn't seem like they were.

And I remembered them, which more than likely meant that the Jewel up there hadn't gotten complete control over my mind. I had been lucky this time.

"You're bleeding," Barb said, seeming almost surprised.

I glanced down at my shoulder. Where my costume had been ripped I could see raw skin where the brick on that wall I hit had sanded my skin down more layers than was healthy. I moved my arm around a little. It hurt, but it would still work for me. At least nothing was seriously damaged. As hard as I had hit that building, it might have been. Of course, without hitting the building, I would have been very dead on the sidewalk.

"I heal quickly," I said to her. "Don't worry about it."

She nodded, still looking concerned.

Hawkins put his gun away and moved to stand beside Barb. Drew stayed back.

"What happened up there?" Hawkins asked. "One second you were looking in a window and the next instant you were nothing more than a falling body."

I quickly went back over what had gone on, right up to where I had purposely smacked myself into the side of the building to knock his control lose.

"Man, I don't remember any green eyes," Drew said, holstering his gun and moving up beside his partner.

"I think I remember because he didn't have complete control over me when I hit that wall."

Drew sort of nodded.

"So we know how he was getting his zombies," Barb said. "All he had to do was look at them while riding the subway."

"Seems that way," I said, remembering the Jewel's green, glowing eyes and shuddering. The zombies who didn't remember were lucky. I was going to have to live with the image of those green eyes for the rest of my life.

"So where'd he get this power?" Hawkins asked.

"Maybe he just grew into it," I said, frowning. "Right now we have to focus on stopping him."

Barb lightly touched my good shoulder. I guess having green snakes crawl around inside my head and banging into a wall had made me a little testy.

"You're right," Hawkins said, not noticing. "You've seen the layout up there. Any ideas?"

"None," I said.

"I still think gas might work," Drew said. "You knock the guy out and he can't look at you. Right?"

"No delivery system," Hawkins said.

I glanced at Sergeant Drew, then back at his partner. "You know, Drew might have something there."

"What are you thinking?" Barb asked.

I really didn't much like what I was thinking, but at this point I didn't see a choice. Any plan was better than no plan.

"A real powerful gas, flooding those penthouse rooms," I said, "just might do the trick."

"And how do we get it up there?" Hawkins said. "I'm not sending a helicopter anywhere close to those windows if what you said about his eyes is even half right."

"I'll take it," I said. "I should be able to get the gas in and get out before he even knows I'm around."

I couldn't believe I was agreeing to go back up there, into that snake-pit of a penthouse. But the words had come out of my mouth and it was too late to back out now. No matter how much I wanted to.

Hawkins shook his head at me. "You do like the punishment, don't you?"

"I don't plan on reaching free fall velocity again in my escape," I said.

"And you planned that the first time?" Barb said. "I'm impressed."

I glanced at her. She was smiling and I had absolutely no comeback. I hated when she did that to me. And she did it to me a lot.

HERE WE GO AGAIN

It took Hawkins and Drew about an hour to get me ready for my next attack on the penthouse. The map of the penthouse they had gotten from the hotel manager showed ten different rooms, all connected by doors. The entire place was like a giant square doughnut with the center being the elevator and maintenance shafts. It was possible to move in a circle around and around inside that place.

Drew rigged me up so that I had eleven gas grenades in a pack on my back. Each grenade was about the size of a large hot dog and had a remote-control timer built in. Drew showed me how to set it to go off in three seconds if I needed to. Otherwise, I would trigger them all at once from a button they strapped on a belt around my waist. When I triggered the gas grenades in the apartment, Hawkins would also flood the stairs and the elevator shafts, just to make sure he had no where to go. The snipers would be watching for him to come out on one of the balconies.

"Any limit on the range of this trigger?" I asked, adjusting the pack to make sure it was secure.

"Half mile," Drew said. "We can fire them when you get back down here if you want."

"Fine idea by me," I said.

"Just make sure you get them as far into each room as you can, and high up if you can. This is a heavy gas. It will flood a twenty by twenty area solidly and then drop."

"Strong stuff, I hope."

Drew smiled. Almost an evil smile, like a child playing with a favorite toy and telling its secrets. "Don't worry," Drew said. "He gets a lung full and he won't be moving around for hours."

"You just be sure to not breath it either," Barb said.

"I'll do my best," I said. "Anything else I should know?"

"Can't think of a thing," Drew said.

Hawkins just shook his head. "You're totally nuts."

"I've been told that before," I said. "Just make sure you remember your promise to me."

"My men all have their orders."

"Time to go smoke a rat out of its hole," I said.

I quickly moved across the street and jumped to the side of the hotel. A few seconds later I was back on the roof of the penthouse.

I used my spider-sense to generally spot in which room of the penthouse the Jewel was in. Then I moved to the other side and dropped down onto a patio.

As quietly as I possibly could under the circumstances, I yanked open one door, ripping the lock right out of the wall. The room inside was a second bedroom. The bed was made and the room looked as if it were waiting for a customer. It didn't look as if the Jewel ever came in here at all.

I put an armed gas grenade inside the ceiling light anyway, then tried to figure out which door to go through. I knew from the plans that one door went into a bathroom while the other door lead into a larger family-type room.

My spider-sense told me there was no danger behind either, so I opened the bathroom door and left it open to make sure the gas got in there. No point in wasting a grenade that just might come in handy later. Then I went through the other door into what the plans called a game room.

It had books on the walls and a pool table on one side. This place was also neat and clean, again as if the Jewel never came into this part of the penthouse either. I put the armed gas grenade on top of the light over the pool table.

I looked around, feeling very much like a common thief casing out a place to rob. This wasn't at all my normal way of doing business. I liked wading into a fight, cracking jokes and hitting bad guys. This sneaking around stuff just wasn't my style.

But fighting snakes inside my head wasn't my style either. So for the moment, this would have to work because slugging it out with this guy just wasn't an option.

There were two doors on the far side of the game room. One led into another bedroom.

Same routine: armed grenade on top of the light.

The second door went into a short hall. At the end of that hall I knew was a second door into the master bedroom where the Jewel slept. I put one armed grenade in the light fixture of the hall, then listened with both my ears and my spider-sense to see if he was in his bedroom.

As far as I could tell, he wasn't.

I moved in and put another armed gas grenade in the cord holding the light to the ceiling right over the bed, then another above a chest in the master bathroom.

My next stop was the pizza-box graveyard of the dining area. I could sense that I was getting closer to him. I thought for a moment about just going back on the roof and tossing the grenades through the windows while setting them off. Safer plan.

But not as effective.

I moved through the door and into the dining room.

My spider-sense danger warning got more intense. He was in the next room, more than likely still sitting at the desk. And if he'd just stay right there for another minute or so, I'd have this part of the penthouse all ready to light up.

I climbed up on the table and eased an armed grenade onto the light fixture. I was just about to try to climb silently down through the jungle of Coke cups and dried-up pizza boxes when my spider-sense went totally wild.

He was coming into the room.

And I was standing on his dining table.

In the middle of all his pizza boxes.

That would make just about anyone mad.

Not good.

Not good at all.

"What?" I heard him say.

"Time to clear the table," I said.

I took two quick steps on the huge table, keeping my eyes closed so I would take no chance of even catching a reflected glimpse of him, and then dove headfirst through the window.

The glass shattered around me and I dropped out over the street.

Without looking back I twisted around in mid-air and fired a web at the corner of the building with one hand while pushing the trigger for the gas grenades I had set in the penthouse. If he was still in that dining room, he was going to get a lung full of gas.

Inside the top floor of the hotel I heard the muffled soft sounds of the grenades going off.

Perfect.

I swung around to the other side of the building and quickly climbed back up to the roof. There I triggered another grenade and tossed it through the glass of the window into the office where the money was stacked. I watched it roll on the floor, spewing its poison as my spider-sense warned me to get back.

I listened.

I quickly moved to the next window and did the same, hoping I had trapped him in the office area. If he was trying to run from the gas, I'd chase him right into the rooms already full.

Three more gas grenades through windows and I was out of ammunition.

I quickly moved back up to the center of the roof of the penthouse and waited. The gas was seeping out of windows and blowing out of doors and the windows I'd broken. From what I could tell, the entire suite of rooms had been flooded.

But my spider-sense told me there was still great danger below me. If he was knocked out, I would have known it. My spider-sense wouldn't have been warning me.

Something had gone wrong.

Could he have found a place in there that was gas free? I was sure I had covered every room, either from the inside or through a window.

I sat and waited, crouched behind a large roof fan as shelter from the cold wind. My spider-sense didn't dim at all. He was still down there.

Still walking and moving around.

And still just as dangerous.

The gas had failed.

Now what?

I moved over to the edge of the penthouse on the side my spider-sense told me he wasn't, then dove off the roof, making sure my eyes were closed as I passed the penthouse windows.

Two stories down I used a few web shots to swing me down to the street, ending up landing beside Barb, Sergeant Hawkins, and Sergeant Drew.

"We flooded the elevators and stairwells when you blew the grenades," Drew said.

"How'd it go?" Barb asked.

"The operation was a success," I said, "but the patient lived."

"You want to say that in English?" Hawkins said.

"We filled the entire penthouse with gas as far as I can figure. But he's still up there and moving around. The gas didn't knock him out for some reason or another."

"Are you sure?" Barb asked.

"I'm sure," I said. I looked at the stunned faces of all three of them. "Anyone have a plan B?"

No one spoke up.

Chapter Seventeen
Going In Again

For most of the last hour Barb and I had been standing in a doorway, out of the wind, staring at the front of the Crown Plaza Hotel. It now seemed a long time since our failed gas attack. After about a half hour I'd gone back to the roof to see if he was still moving around in there.

He had been.

Somehow, either using a gas mask, or with his powers, he had escaped our attack. And now none of us had any ideas what to do next, except wait.

"We have this guy outnumbered three hundred to one and can't get him off that building. I find that somewhat amazing, actually," I said.

Barb shook her head.

"What bothers me," she said, "and what I keep coming back to, is how he got that power."

She paced back and forth as she talked, her heavy coat blowing in the wind every time she turned around. "Somehow I feel that's the key to all this."

"I've known dozens of super-villains over the years and that question just doesn't come up much," I said, joking with her.

She ignored me, lost in a train of thought as she paced. "I keep going back to the lab report on the residue from that spot in the alley. And then your description of the Jewel's eyes. Glowing I think you said."

The memory of those eyes overwhelmed me, as if the Jewel was trying to take me over again. No snakes this time. Just huge, glowing eyes that seemed to want to swallow me, pull me into their cold light. It was going to be a long, long time before I forgot those eyes.

I shook off the image and tried to focus on what Barb was saying. Maybe she was making sense. "You think the Jewel killed Bobby and picked up what was in that alley?" I asked. "And whatever he picked up gave him these powers?"

"There haven't been any reports of radiation poisoning or death the last two weeks," she said. "Yet someone picked up what was there. You read the lab report. You tell me if that is possible."

"Anything is possible," I said.

I tried to focus my tired mind on what I remembered from that report. It had said the radiation was very intense. And dangerous. And that the type was unknown combination. I had gotten my powers from the bite of a radioactive spider. I knew of even stranger things being caused by radiation.

Right then I knew what I needed to do next. "I think it's about time I find out if your theory is right or not. Better than waiting, don't you think?"

"Find out?" Barb said. "How?"

"By searching his room," I said. "How else?"

"You can't do that."

I ignored her and started across the street toward the hotel. "Tell Hawkins what I'm going after. And if I were you, I'd have Hawkins get some gieger counters here quick."

"What exactly *are* you going after?"

"I don't know exactly," I said, over my shoulder. "But chances are it'll be radioactive, it melts snow in alleys, and I'll know it when I see it."

She had no response. I had finally gotten the last word with her. I just hoped it wasn't my *very* last word.

I went up the side of the hotel and was quickly back on the roof of the penthouse. I really didn't have a plan. I was mostly just tired of waiting. It was starting to get dark and I needed food and a good night's sleep more than anything else in the world. The only way I was going to get that was to take care of this nutcase once and for all.

And clear those green eyes out of my mind.

"Okay, Spidey old man," I said out loud, letting the wind take my words off into the gray sky, "you're here. Now what?"

The wind didn't answer.

I moved around the roof until my spider-sense told me the Jewel was in the office again where the money had been stacked. I would bet anything that the thing that had caused the radiation in the alley was in that room, right there with the money.

If Barb's theory was right.

At this point, after the last two weeks, I was hoping she was.

But I had to get him out of that room before I could go inside and find out.

I went to a window on the opposite side of the penthouse. It looked in on the game room. If I could somehow lure him there, that would give me a few seconds to get back to the office and look around.

I fired a web at the corner of the roof and then with a running leap swung out into the air over the street.

The web brought me back around at just the right point and I went through the window feet first, smashing the glass. I hit and rolled under the pool table.

"Perfect," I said, my voice hollow in the empty room. I stood and lifted the pool table, letting it smash down on its side with a crash that I bet shook the entire penthouse.

"Hey Green Eyes!" I shouted as loud as I could. "How about a rematch!"

My shout echoed through the penthouse and my spider-sense could tell he was moving, heading this way.

"Bring on those snake eyes of yours!" I shouted at the top of my lungs, then dove as silently as possible back through the broken window.

I let myself fall a few floors to make sure I was out of his sight, then caught the edge of the building with a web in such a way that it swung me around the corner and back up just under the penthouse office window.

My spider-sense, because it wasn't buzzing, told me he wasn't in the room.

My little pool table diversion had worked. But I didn't have long.

I went in through the broken window of the dining room and moved immediately through the door between the two rooms and into the office.

The place looked the same as before, except for the spent gas grenade against the wall. The money was still stacked on the corner of the desk with the Sandpines hat on top of it.

"Drafty," I said softly to myself as a slight wind blew through the small hole in the window from the grenade. "Got to be hard to heat this."

I moved quickly behind the desk. A yellow legal pad was on the top of the desk. The top sheet was blank.

I couldn't help myself.

I quickly wrote on it: *Are we having fun yet?*

And I signed it *Spider-Man.*

My spider-sense told me the Jewel was still two rooms away in the game room.

"Okay, where would you keep something radioactive?"

I opened the top desk drawer.

"Bingo."

There, just as simple as can be, in the pen tray was a green stone about the size of my thumb. It looked like an emerald, only this one glowed just like the Jewel's eyes.

Cold green light.

"Now I see where you got your name," I said. "Cute."

My spider-sense went totally wild.

"Glad you think so," a deep voice said from the other room as the door on the far side opened.

The Jewel was coming back and he knew I was here. I had no time.

Hoping my gloves would save me from the radiation, I grabbed the emerald from the desk and threw it through the hole in the window left by the gas grenade.

Perfect strike.

The green stone arched out over the street.

Then I did a rolling dive over the desk.

"What's the hurry?" the Jewel said. His voice was deep, inviting.

Too inviting.

The green snakes in my mind seemed to be back.

Moving.

Trying to get me to stay.

To look at him.

Not to run.

I sprang as hard as I could at the window.

I had to get away.

Another second and it would be too late.

With my shoulder I hit the window as hard as I had the one in the dining room, smashing the glass outward.

"My jewel!" he shouted as I cleared the window and he entered the room. "You've stolen my jewel!"

The pain and jarring of hitting the window banished the snakes from my head again. It was like waking up again from a long night's sleep.

"It's on the street below," I shouted back as I fell. "Come and get it."

I broke my fall two stories down with a web and quickly worked my way down to the street.

Barb was running for the place where the emerald had fallen.

As I dropped down beside her she pointed at the green gem melting a hole in the snow near the curb. Powerful radiation to be that physically hot. More than likely we shouldn't even be standing close to it.

"Geiger counters on the way," she said. "And radiation gear."

"You were right," I said. "Tell Hawkins and Drew that the Jewel is on his way down. And he's not happy."

"What about this thing," she said, pointing at the emerald. "We can't take a chance of him getting it again."

"And what would you suggest doing with it? We don't dare touch it."

"The same thing I hope to do to him for killing Bobby," Barb said.

The big gun was out from under her coat almost as fast as an eye could follow.

She pointed it at the emerald.

My spider-sense went wild.

"No!" I shouted and tried to knock the gun aside by jumping in front of her.

I was too late.

Just an instant too late.

And she was a good shot.

A very good shot, in fact.

The emerald exploded like a massive bomb going off.

One instant I was reaching for her gun, trying to stop her from firing, and the next I was flying through the air, tumbling like a rag doll tossed by an angry child.

My instincts were to try to stop the tumble, hit anything with a web shot to stabilize myself.

But there was no time.

I was too stunned from the blast and traveling too fast.

I hit the side of the hotel about twenty feet up the brick wall.

And this time I just didn't graze it. I hit it head on.

Hard.

Harder than I have hit anything in my memory. And I have a very good memory for such hits to my body.

The impact knocked the wind out of me.

I dropped like a bag of sand face first onto the sidewalk. My face ground down into the salt someone had sprinkled there to keep the snow off.

"Ouch," I whispered. I didn't have enough wind left in me to do anything but whisper.

I laid there as the world spun behind my eyes.

Flashes of light.

Green snake eyes.

Flashes of light.

More green eyes.

Over and over.

Around and around and around.

The sound of the explosion was still ringing in my ears and echoing off through the buildings.

All I wanted was for the spinning to stop.

Around and around everything went until slowly blackness crept over the green eyes and the bright flashes.

And then everything went around and around right down into a deep, black hole.

THOSE NIGHTMARES ARE BREAKING UP THAT OLD DREAM OF MINE

It was an awful nightmare.

I was riding on the back of a huge green snake, holding onto the back of its head trying to keep it from turning and biting me.

Bright light shot out of the snake's eyes as it bucked and slithered and rolled and did everything to get me off. But I wouldn't let go.

I rode like a true champion, spurs and all, until the snake dipped into the ice and water of the river. Then my hands and face got cold.

And my back hurt.

And I could hear someone calling me.

So I let go.

The snake hit me with its tail, flipping me out of the river.

The only thing close enough for me to try to web to break my fall were huge green eyes.

But my web kept slipping off the eyes.

And the voice kept calling me. "Spidey? Spider-Man? Can you hear me?"

Finally I punched one of the huge eyes and they all blew up, sending green blood over the entire city.

Flooding everything.

The eye exploding smashed me into a sidewalk.

And then I was awake.

Laying face down on something very hard and cold.

Awful nightmare.

Awful.

And this bed was hard, too. Maybe I was still dreaming?

"Spider-Man?"

I opened one eye.

Snow.

Piles of snow and concrete.

What a weird place to take a nap.

Then I saw the shoes. Cop shoes.

It took me a moment to remember. I was on the sidewalk in front of the Crown Plaza Hotel. Okay, got that much.

Now what? How had I gotten here?

Barb had shot at the emerald.

It had exploded.

Got it.

I opened both eyes and tried to sit up.

Someone's firm hands tried to help. Between the two of us we managed to get my body sitting upright, even though my head felt as if it were being spun on a carnival ride.

A really fast ride at that. With lots of great lights.

I blinked a few times and focused on the face of Sergeant Drew as it spun past.

"Glad to see you're back with us," Drew said, smiling.

"How long?" I asked, my voice sounding odd to my ears. Distant and muffled. More than likely from the explosion.

"Were you out?" Drew asked.

I tried to nod and instantly regretted it as the swirling got worse and the carnival ride picked up speed around the inside of my head..

"Only about thirty seconds," he said. "As long as it took me to run to you."

"Barb?"

"Don't know," he said, suddenly looking worried. "You blocked most of the blast when you jumped in front of her. She was blown across the street and landed in a snow bank. Hawkins is with her. What exploded anyway?"

I motioned for him to wait just a moment, then I took a long, slow, deep breath that seemed to help the spinning a little.

A second long breath helped even more. And cleared my ears a little too.

By the third I was ready to try to move.

"It was an emerald, about the size of your thumb. I think it was where the Jewel got his powers."

"So what made it explode?"

"Barb shot it."

"Oh," Drew said. "Do emeralds always explode when shot?"

"How should I know," I said. "Help me up, would you?"

"Sure," Drew said.

I stood slowly, letting the spinning do its thing while I steadied myself on the strong shoulder of the sergeant.

"Amazing," Drew said. "That smash into the wall would have killed anyone else. You hit about two floors up."

"Hard to kill a Spider-Man," I said.

Drew laughed. "Yeah, I guess so."

"Trust me," I said. "It still hurts."

"I'll bet."

Carefully, we headed toward where Barb was being attended to in the snow drift.

She looked awful. She had cuts on her arms and legs, and her coat was in tatters. And she was unconscious. But she was still alive.

"Ambulance on the way," Hawkins said as we got close. He looked very worried. "What happened?"

While leaning on Drew's shoulder I quickly told him what had happened up in the penthouse and what Barb had done shooting the thing.

Hawkins only nodded.

I let go of Drew's shoulder and took a few more deep breaths. The dizziness was clearing. I hurt in about twenty places I knew of at the moment. And for certain, tomorrow morning there would be at least another twenty more aches. But I was alive and so was Barb. That's what mattered the most.

We were lucky.

There was a thirty-foot crater in the middle of the street where the emerald had exploded to remind us just how lucky we really were. And not a window within the entire block on the ground floor was intact.

"Sergeant," I said to Drew.

"Yeah?" he said, moving quickly beside me.

"I think you need to get this crater blocked off. It could be extremely radioactive," I said.

"Already checked it," Hawkins said from beside Barb. "And we checked her. No radiation at all."

I had no idea how that was possible, but for the moment it was the first lucky break we had gotten.

"Any sign of the Jewel coming yet?"

"Nothing," Drew said. "Everyone's standing ready. If he came straight down he should have been out here by now."

I nodded. "I'd suggest you get a few men down here right now to start searching this area for any part of that emerald that might be left. Even if the area isn't radioactive, the emerald pieces are. Tell them to use geiger counters and not to touch it if they find anything. I'll go see if I can spot where the Jewel is at."

"You sure you're up for that?" Hawkins asked.

"You want to go in there looking for him?"

"No," he said.

"Then just take care of her. I'll figure out what happened to our green-eyed friend. Keep everyone on alert."

"Oh, they are," Hawkins said. "And after you took his jewel namesake, he's going to be even angrier."

"Count on it," I said.

I headed back across the street toward the hotel. The spinning in my head was still there, but clearing fast. And in the distance I could again hear the normal sounds of the city, which meant my hearing was almost back too.

I stopped on the sidewalk near where I had landed and double-checked my web-shooters to make sure they hadn't been damaged. Luckily, they were fine.

"Okay, Spidey old boy," I said aloud. "Once more into the breach."

Going slower than I normally would, I started back up the outside of the Crown Plaza Hotel. It was a much longer climb than I had remembered.

DEAD EYES

I was standing in the center of the penthouse roof taking deep breaths of the cold wind before I realized what was different. My spider-sense wasn't warning me of the danger.

Maybe the explosion and bang on the head had knocked it out of whack? That was possible. As bad as I felt at the moment, that was more than likely.

Yet I knew that the two spider-tracers were still down there in the penthouse, stuck to the money bags. I could sense them.

But I couldn't sense any danger. Was the Jewel gone?

Was he down on the street?

I eased down the wall between the windows of the penthouse dining room and office. I had dove out of both windows over the last few hours and now the wind blew the drapes like flags, snapping them back and forth.

My spider-sense was clear.

Or, thanks to the emerald, broken. Too many weird things concerning that emerald had happed. If it could explode and not leave any radiation anything could be possible.

I eased myself closer to the edge of the dining room window and peeked inside.

Clear.

The wind had blown the pizza boxes against the far wall and spilled Coke all over the table.

I moved over to the office window and peaked inside.

The Jewel was sitting behind his desk, his head down on the desk. The money had been blown all over the room and his yellow legal pad was fluttering in the wind near the door.

There was a low moaning coming from the room, but I couldn't be sure if it was the wind or not.

My spider-sense told me the man was not dangerous.

Could I dare trust it? How could he not be dangerous? That made no sense.

I held onto the side of the wall with only one hand so it would be easy to let go and drop away if my spider-sense warned me to, or if he tried to get me with those green eyes again.

Then I leaned out over the shattered window and said, "Hey Jewel boy. Didn't they ever tell you crime bosses don't sleep?"

He didn't change position.

I could see him breathing, so I knew he was still alive.

I waited, expecting a trap.

Money fluttered in the wind around the room.

The Sandpines golf hat hung from the side of the desk, a hundred dollar bill stuck in it.

The guy didn't move.

"I'll tell you a joke," I shouted at him. "No one can sit still for my jokes."

He didn't move.

"I hate one-sided conversations," I said.

With a quick web shot, I covered the top of his head and pulled.

Like a wet rag, he came over the top of the desk, flipped over in mid-air, and landed flat on his back in the middle of the room.

I almost dropped away, thinking his flip move was a trap. Then I caught a glimpse of his eyes.

Or more accurately where his eyes had been.

Now there were only charred black holes in his face.

Like the eyes of a skeleton.

His hands came up and he put his fingers in the holes.

And then he screamed.

And screamed and screamed.

The sound carried out over the city, signaling the end of the crime wave.

The case was solved.

The emerald was destroyed.

And so was the Jewel.

Chapter Eighteen
A Short Good-bye

I was back on the street just as the ambulance carrying Barb pulled away. The crater in the street was already taped off and men in heavy yellow radiation suits were working the edges of it.

"How is she?" I asked Hawkins.

"They said she's going to make it."

"Good," was the only thing I could think to say. The relief felt almost like a fist to the stomach. I hadn't realized over the last ten minutes how much I was worried about her.

"So where's the Jewel?" Hawkins asked.

"In his office up there," I said. "But he's defanged, or I guess I should say de-eyed."

Hawkins and Drew both looked at me with puzzled expressions on their cop faces. And puzzled expressions is something you never want to see on a cop.

"Don't worry. He's safe," I said. "It's all over. Call off your men except for the ones who are going to meet us upstairs to arrest what's left of him."

"How'd you finally stop him?" Drew asked.

"I didn't," I said. "Barb did. With one shot I might add."

Again they both looked at me strangely. I waved them off. "I'll explain it all later. Right now you've got someone to arrest up there and a mess to clear up down here. I'll meet you up there."

"Right," Hawkins said and they both turned and headed for the hotel front door.

I had enough sense to head back up the side of the building one more time and get my camera out of my pack where I had hid it on the roof. I snapped five or six quick shots of the inside of the Jewel's penthouse, plus four of the Jewel himself laying on the carpet. He'd terrorized the entire city for two full weeks, killed eight people, and wounded hundreds more,

201

not counting almost destroying hundreds of more lives by turning them into armed crooks. The city had a right to see what it had gotten him in return.

I had my camera back in my pack before the cops got the elevators turned back on and got to the penthouse.

I hung around for the next hour but no one found even one sliver of the emerald, which, of course, wasn't possible if it had simply exploded. Something else must have happened to it.

I remembered a while back the X-Men had dealt with some jewels connected with the one that gave the Juggernaut his powers. So after leaving the hotel, I found a phone and made a call.

X-Men mansion.

Professor Xavier called the gemstones they had delt with the Jewels of Cyttorak. He told me they, except for the one in the Juggernaut's chest, had vanished in an explosion, also.

And yes, one was an emerald.

The only other thing the Professor would tell me after I gave him the entire story, including the radiation break-down from the alley, was that the emerald was more than likely one of the Jewels of Cyttorak. And more than likely it had arrived and vanished through time when shot.

"Thus the explosion with nothing left and no radiation," I said.

"Actually, an implosion that sucked the emerald, radiation, and most of the immediate area into the time vaccuum hole it created," he said. "You were lucky not to get pulled in, as well."

He went on to tell me there was no telling when or where it might appear again. And there was nothing anyone on this Earth could do to change that.

I thanked him and was glad to hang up.

At least I had one possible answer for where the emerald had come from. It had more than likely appeared in that alley from out of time. And when Barb shot it, it went through time again, taking the Jewel's powers with it.

I hoped it was in a place a long ways off. Both in time and distance.

Around eight I managed to get home, change into a new Spider-Man suit and have Mary Jane make sure that dressed as Peter Parker I didn't show any bad damage. Luckily I didn't. At least nothing was turning black and blue yet. I'm sure it would.

I had a little snack with a promise that I would return for a bigger dinner shortly. I still had two more stops to make before this was finished completely.

The first was back to the *Bugle*.

The newsroom was like a wild party, with everyone working and happy.

"Peter!" Robbie shouted across the newsroom as he came out of his office, a broad smile on his face. "Tell me you got pictures."

I held up my camera pack. "Thirty minutes."

He gave me a huge grin and the thumbs up sign, then went back to his desk.

I had the pictures developed in twenty-one minutes. The close-up of the Jewel's face at first shocked Robbie. He sat behind his desk staring at it.

It took me a full forty-five minutes to relay what I had "learned" from Spider-Man to Robbie and two reporters. Then it was as if I didn't exist as they headed to put the morning paper together and write the news that would have the city cheering tomorrow morning.

My second stop was as Spider-Man at the hospital.

I had learned by calling from the *Bugle* which room Barb was in. I actually went in the front door, getting stares all the way. I'd had my share today of going in and out of windows. Even the strange looks in the hallways were better at the moment.

An elderly couple rode up on the elevator with me. They stood to one side and kept staring at me sideways, as if they couldn't decide to run or scream.

About halfway to Barb's floor, the elderly woman finally turned to me, looking me up and down as if I was a side of beef. "Are you that Spider-Person?"

"I am," I said.

She didn't look happy. "The one that swings between the buildings?"

"I do that," I said, trying to be as nice as I could. I didn't want to scare her at all.

"Humph," she said, clearly disgusted. She turned back to stare at the elevator door, her chin in the air.

"See, Angel," the man said, patting her shoulder. "I told you he wasn't very tall."

I was so shocked that the doors to the elevator opened and the couple shuffled off before I could even close my mouth.

Hawkins and Drew had both managed to finish their work around the hotel and beat me to the hospital. Hawkins stood beside the bed and Drew was stretched out in a chair, his feet up on the end table.

Barb was sitting up, two or three pillows propped behind her. Her hair was pulled back and she had a large bandage on her forehead and a swollen right eye. But otherwise she looked fine.

"I was wondering if you were going to come by," she said, smiling at me. "We had the window open and everything."

"Glad you're all right," I said.

"Thanks to you," she said. "Your body took most of the blast. That saved my life."

"I wish everyone I saved was as good-looking as you. Most look like Sergeant Drew here."

She laughed. Then her eyes got serious. "Thank you."

"You are more than welcome," I said, just as serious. Only behind my mask she couldn't see my eyes. I just hoped my voice told her clearly enough.

For the next half hour the four of us talked about what had happened. I learned that the Jewel's real name was Charlie David, a small-time crook with a record of robberies as long as my arm. He was known for not being very bright.

Thank heavens for that. If a truly smart crook had gotten his hands on that emerald, with those powers, there would have been no stopping him. Ever.

I also learned from Barb that Hawkins had found a gun in the drawer in the penthouse that matched the type used to kill Bobby in that alley. She was betting the tests tomorrow would prove it was the same one. None of us took that bet because Hawkins then told me what good old Charlie David, aka "The Jewel", had told him after they got him to stop screaming.

It seems that Charlie had been walking down the street, minding his own business when a small explosion happened in the alley where Bobby was staked out, sending a green flash through the snow.

"The emerald arriving through time," I said.

"What?" Barb said.

I quickly explained to them what I knew from the X-Men, then told Hawkins to go on with what the Jewel had said.

"From the way it looked, Bobby had just been in the wrong place at the wrong time," Drew said. "He was in the alley working for Barb on the furniture scam stakeout when the emerald arrived, as you say, through time."

"From the tracks in the snow," Hawkins said, "we know Bobby went to look at the emerald. Good old petty thief Charlie David came into the alley and saw it too. He got greedy, drew a gun and shot Bobby for it."

"Then he was stupid enough to touch something that was glowing green and melting snow," I said.

"Exactly," Hawkins said.

"Bobby was just the first victim of the Jewel," Barb said. "And like all the others, he was just in the wrong place at the wrong time."

How right she was about that.

We kept talking for the next half hour, going over the details of the case again. Finally, just about the time I was starting to think about that wonderful dinner waiting for me, followed by my warm bed, a male nurse with a nasty frown came in and threatened to call the police if we didn't let this woman get some sleep.

Drew flashed his badge at the nurse, who only frowned.

"I mean real police."

Both Barb and I found that just a little too funny. Drew and Hawkins didn't.

Instead of chancing another ride on that elevator, I decided to use the window. I got it open and was crouched there, the nurse frowning at me when Barb stopped me.

"Spider-Man, promise you'll return tomorrow," she said. "They're going to hold me for two days just to make sure everything is all right. Trust me, I'm going to be bored."

Crouched in the cold night air I looked back at her. "Oh, so now I've gone from being just another pretty face to entertainment."

She laughed. "My dear Spider-Man, you always were entertainment."

I laughed. "I think that's the nicest thing you've ever said to me."

With that I turned and jumped from the window, firing a web to swing off over the street below.

Behind me I heard her say, "And that should worry you, don't you think?"

Again she had gotten the last line. With a woman like her, a man could get a real inferiority complex.

A justified one.

AUTHOR'S NOTE TO THE READER

For the complete origin story of the emerald, read the novel *X-Men: The Jewels of Cyttorak.*

Dean Wesley Smith has sold over one hundred professional short stories and twenty-five novels, but he claims that, since he was a comics fan for years, his favorites, like this volume, are based on comics. He has written the Spider-Man novels *Carnage in New York* (coauthored with David Michelinie) and *Goblin's Revenge*, and the X-Men novel *The Jewels of Cyttorak*, which is the prequel of this book. Smith has also written the young-adult novel *Iron Man Super Thriller: Steel Terror* and the novelization of the movie *Steel*. With award-winning author Kristine Kathryn Rusch he cowrote the novelization of the hit movie *X-Men*. Smith has also published novels under his own name and under the name Sandy Schofield in the *Star Trek* and *Aliens* series. Smith has also collaborated with *Star Trek: The Next Generation*'s Jonathan Frakes. Smith has won the World Fantasy Award and has been nominated numerous times for the Hugo Award and the Nebula Award.

Bob Hall has been illustrating comics for both Marvel and DC since the 1970s. In addition, Hall has been a theatrical producer and was the producer of the successful off-Broadway play *The Passion of Dracula*. Hall was an editor at Marvel during the 1970s. He was the illustrator of the Marvel graphic novel *Emperor Doom*. Presently he is illustrating a Batman miniseries for DC.

CHRONOLOGY TO THE MARVEL NOVELS
AND ANTHOLOGIES

What follows is a guide to the order in which the Marvel novels and short stories published by BP Books, Inc., and Berkley Boulevard Books take place in relation to each other. Please note that this is not a hard and fast chronology, but a guideline that is subject to change at authorial or editorial whim. This list covers all the novels and anthologies published from October 1994–October 2000.

The short stories are each given an abbreviation to indicate which anthology the story appeared in. USM=*The Ultimate Spider-Man*, USS=*The Ultimate Silver Surfer*, USV=*The Ultimate Super-Villains*, UXM=*The Ultimate X-Men*, UTS=*Untold Tales of Spider-Man*, UH=*The Ultimate Hulk*, and XML=*X-Men Legends*.

X-Men & Spider-Man: Time's Arrow Book 1: **The Past [portions]** by Tom DeFalco & Jason Henderson
Parts of this novel take place in prehistoric times, the sixth century, 1867, and 1944.

"The Silver Surfer" [flashback] by Tom DeFalco & Stan Lee [USS]
The Silver Surfer's origin. The early parts of this flashback start several decades, possibly several centuries, ago, and continue to a point just prior to "To See Heaven in a Wild Flower."

"In the Line of Banner" by Danny Fingeroth [UH]
This takes place over several years, ending approximately nine months before the birth of Robert Bruce Banner.

X-Men: Codename Wolverine ["then" portions] by Christopher Golden

"Every Time a Bell Rings" by Brian K. Vaughan [XML]
These take place while Team X was still in operation, while the Black Widow was still a Russian spy, while Banshee was still with Interpol, and a couple of years before the X-Men were formed.

"Spider-Man" by Stan Lee & Peter David [USM]
A retelling of Spider-Man's origin.

"Transformations" by Will Murray [UH]
"Side by Side with the Astonishing Ant-Man!" by Will Murray [UTS]
"Assault on Avengers Mansion" by Richard C. White & Steven A. Roman [UH]
"Suits" by Tom De Haven & Dean Wesley Smith [USM]
"After the First Death . . . " by Tom DeFalco [UTS]
"Celebrity" by Christopher Golden & José R. Nieto [UTS]
"Pitfall" by Pierce Askegren [UH]
"Better Looting Through Modern Chemistry" by John Garcia & Pierce Askegren [UTS]
These stories take place very early in the careers of Spider-Man and the Hulk.

"To the Victor" by Richard Lee Byers [USV]
Most of this story takes place in an alternate timeline, but the jumping-off point is here.

"To See Heaven in a Wild Flower" by Ann Tonsor Zeddies [USS]

"Point of View" by Len Wein [USS]
These stories take place shortly after the end of the flash-back portion of "The Silver Surfer."

CHRONOLOGY

"Identity Crisis" by Michael Jan Friedman [UTS]
"The Doctor's Dilemma" by Danny Fingeroth [UTS]
"Moving Day" by John S. Drew [UTS]
"Out of the Darkness" by Glenn Greenberg [UH]
"The Liar" by Ann Nocenti [UTS]
"Diary of a False Man" by Keith R.A. DeCandido [XML]
"Deadly Force" by Richard Lee Byers [UTS]
"Truck Stop" by Jo Duffy [UH]
"Hiding" by Nancy Holder & Christopher Golden [UH]
"Improper Procedure" by Keith R.A. DeCandido [USS]
"The Ballad of Fancy Dan" by Ken Grobe & Steven A. Roman [UTS]
"Welcome to the X-Men, Madrox ... " by Steve Lyons [XML]
  These stories take place early in the careers of Spider-Man, the Silver Surfer, the Hulk, and the X-Men, after their origins and before the formation of the "new" X-Men.

"Here There Be Dragons" by Sholly Fisch [UH]
"Peace Offering" by Michael Stewart [XML]
"The Worst Prison of All" by C. J. Henderson [XML]
"Poison in the Soul" by Glenn Greenberg [UTS]
"Do You Dream in Silver?" by James Dawson [USS]
"A Quiet, Normal Life" by Thomas Deja [UH]
"Livewires" by Steve Lyons [UTS]
"Arms and the Man" by Keith R.A. DeCandido [UTS]
"Incident on a Skyscraper" by Dave Smeds [USS]
"A Green Snake in Paradise" by Steve Lyons [UH]
  These all take place after the formation of the "new" X-Men and before Spider-Man got married, the Silver Surfer ended his exile on Earth, and the reemergence of the gray Hulk.

"Cool" by Lawrence Watt-Evans [USM]
"Blindspot" by Ann Nocenti [USM]
"Tinker, Tailor, Soldier, Courier" by Robert L. Washington III [USM]
"Thunder on the Mountain" by Richard Lee Byers [USM]

"The Stalking of John Doe" by Adam-Troy Castro [UTS]
"On the Beach" by John J. Ordover [USS]

These all take place just prior to Peter Parker's marriage to Mary Jane Watson and the Silver Surfer's release from imprisonment on Earth.

Daredevil: Predator's Smile by Christopher Golden
"Disturb Not Her Dream" by Steve Rasnic Tem [USS]
"My Enemy, My Savior" by Eric Fein [UTS]
"Kraven the Hunter Is Dead, Alas" by Craig Shaw Gardner [USM]
"The Broken Land" by Pierce Askegren [USS]
"Radically Both" by Christopher Golden [USM]
"Godhood's End" by Sharman DiVono [USS]
"Scoop!" by David Michelinie [USM]
"The Beast with Nine Bands" by James A. Wolf [UH]
"Sambatyon" by David M. Honigsberg [USS]
"A Fine Line" by Dan Koogler [XML]
"Cold Blood" by Greg Cox [USM]
"The Tarnished Soul" by Katherine Lawrence [USS]
"Leveling Las Vegas" by Stan Timmons [UH]
"Steel Dogs and Englishmen" by Thomas Deja [XML]
"If Wishes Were Horses" by Tony Isabella & Bob Ingersoll [USV]
"The Stranger Inside" by Jennifer Heddle [XML]
"The Silver Surfer" [framing sequence] by Tom DeFalco & Stan Lee [USS]
"The Samson Journals" by Ken Grobe [UH]

These all take place after Peter Parker's marriage to Mary Jane Watson, after the Silver Surfer attained freedom from imprisonment on Earth, before the Hulk's personalities were merged, and before the formation of the X-Men "blue" and "gold" teams.

"The Deviant Ones" by Glenn Greenberg [USV]
"An Evening in the Bronx with Venom" by John Gregory

Betancourt & Keith R.A. DeCandido [USM]
These two stories take place one after the other, and a few months prior to The Venom Factor.

The Incredible Hulk: What Savage Beast by Peter David
This novel takes place over a one-year period, starting here and ending just prior to Rampage.

"Once a Thief" by Ashley McConnell [XML]
"On the Air" by Glenn Hauman [UXM]
"Connect the Dots" by Adam-Troy Castro [USV]
"Ice Prince" by K. A. Kindya [XML]
"Summer Breeze" by Jenn Saint-John & Tammy Lynne Dunn [UXM]
"Out of Place" by Dave Smeds [UXM]
These stories all take place prior to the Mutant Empire *trilogy.*

X-Men: Mutant Empire Book 1: **Siege** by Christopher Golden
X-Men: Mutant Empire Book 2: **Sanctuary** by Christopher Golden
X-Men: Mutant Empire Book 3: **Salvation** by Christopher Golden
These three novels take place within a three-day period.

Fantastic Four: To Free Atlantis by Nancy A. Collins
"The Love of Death or the Death of Love" by Craig Shaw Gardner [USS]
"Firetrap" by Michael Jan Friedman [USV]
"What's Yer Poison?" by Christopher Golden & José R. Nieto [USS]
"Sins of the Flesh" by Steve Lyons [USV]
"Doom²" by Joey Cavalieri [USV]
"Child's Play" by Robert L. Washington III [USV]
"A Game of the Apocalypse" by Dan Persons [USS]

"All Creatures Great and Skrull" by Greg Cox [USV]
"Ripples" by José R. Nieto [USV]
"Who Do You Want Me to Be?" by Ann Nocenti [USV]
"One for the Road" by James Dawson [USV]
   These are more or less simultaneous, with "Doom²" taking place after To Free Atlantis, *"Child's Play" taking place shortly after "What's Yer Poison?" and "A Game of the Apocalypse" taking place shortly after "The Love of Death or the Death of Love."*

"Five Minutes" by Peter David [USM]
   This takes place on Peter Parker and Mary Jane Watson-Parker's first anniversary.

Spider-Man: The Venom Factor by Diane Duane
Spider-Man: The Lizard Sanction by Diane Duane
Spider-Man: The Octopus Agenda by Diane Duane
   These three novels take place within a six-week period.

"The Night I Almost Saved Silver Sable" by Tom DeFalco [USV]
"Traps" by Ken Grobe [USV]
   These stories take place one right after the other.

Iron Man: The Armor Trap by Greg Cox
Iron Man: Operation A.I.M. by Greg Cox
"Private Exhibition" by Pierce Askegren [USV]
Fantastic Four: Redemption of the Silver Surfer by Michael Jan Friedman
Spider-Man & The Incredible Hulk: Rampage (Doom's Day Book 1) by Danny Fingeroth & Eric Fein
Spider-Man & Iron Man: Sabotage (Doom's Day Book 2) by Pierce Askegren & Danny Fingeroth
Spider-Man & Fantastic Four: Wreckage (Doom's Day Book 3) by Eric Fein & Pierce Askegren
   Operation A.I.M. *takes place about two weeks after The*

CHRONOLOGY

Armor Trap. *The Doom's Day trilogy takes place within a three-month period. The events of* Operation A.I.M., *"Private Exhibition,"* Redemption of the Silver Surfer, *and* Rampage *happen more or less simultaneously.* Wreckage *is only a few months after* The Octopus Agenda.

"Such Stuff As Dreams Are Made Of" by Robin Wayne
   Bailey [XML]
"It's a Wonderful Life" by eluki bes shahar [UXM]
"Gift of the Silver Fox" by Ashley McConnell [UXM]
"Stillborn in the Mist" by Dean Wesley Smith [UXM]
"Order from Chaos" by Evan Skolnick [UXM]
   These stories take place more or less simultaneously, with "Such Stuff As Dreams Are Made Of" taking place just prior to the others.

"X-Presso" by Ken Grobe [UXM]
"Life Is But a Dream" by Stan Timmons [UXM]
"Four Angry Mutants" by Andy Lane & Rebecca Levene
   [UXM]
"Hostages" by J. Steven York [UXM]
   These stories take place one right after the other.

Spider-Man: Carnage in New York by David Michelinie &
   Dean Wesley Smith
Spider-Man: Goblin's Revenge by Dean Wesley Smith
   These novels take place one right after the other.

X-Men: Smoke and Mirrors by eluki bes shahar
   This novel takes place three-and-a-half months after "It's a Wonderful Life."

Generation X by Scott Lobdell & Elliot S! Maggin
X-Men: The Jewels of Cyttorak by Dean Wesley Smith

215

Spider-Man: The Gathering of the Sinister Six by Adam-Troy Castro
Generation X: Crossroads by J. Steven York
X-Men: Codename Wolverine ["now" portions] by Christopher Golden
These novels take place one right after the other, with the "now" portions of Codename Wolverine *taking place less than a week after* Crossroads.

The Avengers & the Thunderbolts by Pierce Askegren
Spider-Man: Goblin Moon by Kurt Busiek & Nathan Archer
Nick Fury, Agent of S.H.I.E.L.D.: Empyre by Will Murray
Generation X: Genogoths by J. Steven York
These novels take place at approximately the same time and several months after "Playing It SAFE."

Spider-Man & the Silver Surfer: Skrull War by Steven A. Roman & Ken Grobe
X-Men & the Avengers: Gamma Quest Book 1: **Lost and Found** by Greg Cox
X-Men & the Avengers: Gamma Quest Book 2: **Search and Rescue** by Greg Cox
X-Men & the Avengers: Gamma Quest Book 3: **Friend or Foe?** by Greg Cox
These books take place one right after the other.

X-Men & Spider-Man: Time's Arrow Book 3: **The Future [portions]** by Tom DeFalco & eluki bes shahar
Parts of this novel take place in five different alternate futures in 2020, 2035, 2099, 3000, and the fortieth century.

"The Last Titan" by Peter David [UH]
This takes place in a possible future.

SPIDER-MAN ®